TYLER JOHNSON WAS HERE

JAY COLES

Ⓛ Ⓑ

LITTLE, BROWN AND COMPANY
New York Boston

Little, Brown and Company
Hachette Book Group
1290 Avenue of the Americas, New York, NY 10104
Visit us at LBYR.com

First Edition: March 2018

Little, Brown and Company is a division of Hachette Book Group, Inc. The Little, Brown name and logo are trademarks of Hachette Book Group, Inc.

The publisher is not responsible for websites (or their content) that are not owned by the publisher.

Library of Congress Cataloging-in-Publication Data
Names: Coles, Jay, author.
Title: Tyler Johnson was here / Jay Coles.
Description: First edition. | Boston ; New York : Little, Brown and Company, 2018. | Summary: "When Marvin Johnson's twin brother, Tyler, is shot and killed by a police officer, Marvin must fight injustice to learn the true meaning of freedom" —Provided by publisher.
Identifiers: LCCN 2017027423 | ISBN 9780316440776 (hardcover) | ISBN 9780316440783 (ebook) | ISBN 9780316472197 (library edition ebook)
Subjects: | CYAC: Police shootings—Fiction. | Racism—Fiction. | African Americans—Fiction. | Death—Fiction. | Grief—Fiction. | Brothers—Fiction. | Twins—Fiction. | Single-parent families—Fiction.
Classification: LCC PZ7.1.C6442 Tyl 2018 | DDC [Fic]—dc23
LC record available at https://lccn.loc.gov/2017027423

ISBNs: 978-0-316-44077-6 (hardcover), 978-0-316-44078-3 (ebook)

Printed in the United States of America

LSC-C

10 9 8 7 6 5 4 3 2

To Mom and Grandma,
thank you for always pushing me to
reach for the stars and for showing
me how to speak up

Here's what goes down:

It's just the four of us. My best friends, Ivy and Guillermo (G-mo), my brother, Tyler, and me. We're just strolling through the aisles of a corner convenience store, rapping aloud to my favorite Kendrick Lamar song, "Feel," taking turns rapping verses out loud.

We each choose a bag of chips and a candy bar. For me, I pick salt and vinegar Lay's, something I could toss a mint in my mouth after and still be fine, and then a king-sized Kit Kat bar.

We go up to the register and pay for our stuff. I'm mostly excited to satisfy my growling stomach over a binge marathon of *A Different World*, at my and Tyler's place.

Tyler wouldn't normally be hanging around me and my geek friends, but this is his way of bonding with me. His way of saying *I love you, bro*, even though those words never fall out of his mouth. When we walk out the store, now singing the theme song to *A Different World*, Tyler rolling his eyes and grinning, we realize that we spent too long strolling through the aisles of packaged goods, and by the time we're out the door, the sun has left the sky, the world darkened.

This gets Tyler a little irritated. He checks our shared phone furiously, as if he's expecting an important message or phone call.

Our hood is called Sterling Point. Streetlights smoldering in a fog of cannabis smoke, potholes mazing the roads, gravel driveways, and garden gnomes with bullet holes. Everything is just ugly as shit, except the murals painted out on the sides of walls, black African queens holding their heads high, Tupac staring out with a small smile. But even the ugliness, I guess, is its own kind of beautiful. So I've learned to embrace it.

Tyler, G-mo, and I get on our bikes, and Ivy flips her skateboard right side up. We clutch our snacks to our sides, like they'll somehow get stolen from us on the way back. And when we're a block away from my place, we see a guy walking up our way down the block, turning from Ninth Street. He's dragging his legs, a backpack under his arm.

I slow, and then pump on my handle brakes.

I recognize him. He looks like every other white guy at Sojo High. Skinny. Sad, like he constantly feels out of place. I think I know him from a music theory class I took freshman year. We never talk much outside of class, but we've shared notes.

I've heard all the horror stories of people walking all alone at night ending up missing or something, so I'm about to wave him down—maybe even invite him over to join us for some geeking out over *A Different World*—but all of a sudden, coming out of nowhere, is the striking sound of gunshots. *Pop! Pop! Pop!*

They come in fast and piercing blasts. Again and again.

The skinny white dude drops to the ground, shielding his head.

"What the fuck?" G-mo shouts.

And I fall on my side, my bike slamming down on top of me, crushing my chest on impact with one quick punch.

Everything starts blurring and fading like someone drugged the Kool-Aid I've been sipping on all day from a water bottle. As I lift the bike off me, I feel this huge pang in my head, like I got some sort of goddamn concussion from colliding with the concrete sidewalk.

My next instinct is to stay quiet, to internalize all my cussing and fear, to make sure Ivy, G-mo, and Tyler do the same. It's hard, but I've gotten a lot of training.

I turn over to check on Tyler. Hot Fries are littering his chest, and first they have me thinking they're bloodstains. I furiously search his body for any wounds, almost about to rip off all of his clothing before I finally realize.

He's okay. I'm okay.

G-mo and Ivy are okay.

Their faces are frozen with fear, like the gunshots released all the fear chemicals in their brains. But they're still here.

Man, what the fuck. This shit's straight up got on my last nerve. Why'd they choose tonight for a gang shoot-out?

Then, like, out of nowhere again, I see a cop waddling toward us, and my worst nightmare has started to come true. It isn't a gang shoot-out.

The cop is really pale, skin like a snowfall foreign to Sterling Point—the toilet of America, where shit really goes down. He has a bald head and eyes like the most chilling emeralds. Eyes that scream shitty things at me. *We shouldn't be here.*

He's dragging a boy wearing an all-black hoodie whose hands are being held behind his back—the boy screams in excruciating pain, calling out that he wants to get back home, wailing for the cop to let go of him, that he's unarmed, that he doesn't want to die, and reminding the cop that he's innocent until proven guilty. But the cop isn't hearing that shit.

And so, just ten feet away, he slams the boy on the ground. Suddenly, I'm a little kid again, watching my first body drop from a single bullet, feeling an overwhelming surge of adrenaline. Heart pounding in my chest. Cold sweats sending me shaking.

The cop keeps bashing the poor kid into the sidewalk, smashing his face onto the surface, screaming hate into the back of his head, screaming that he forgot his place in the world, screaming that his wide nose had it coming. All I can see—all I can focus on—is the cop as he pulls out his baton.

And the air I swallow is like Novocain. I go numb all over, adrenaline rising within me. My heart is doing more than beating in my chest—it's rhythmically shredding me. I wonder if I'll return home again. I struggle to remember the last thing I told my mother. Was it something really fucked up? I can't think straight.

The cop's head remains angled down for a while, his baton rising in the air and coming down in rapid, brutal strikes to the back of the poor boy's head. My chest gives in and out, constricting tighter and tighter as each bloody second slips by. I'm stricken with fear.

"What the fuck?!" Ivy screams, hiding her face from the

horror that's going on in front of us. And it's in this moment that the police officer looks over and notices us.

After cuffing the boy underneath him, the cop clutches his gun holster—gives us a glare. "Stay where you are," he says. "Don't fucking move."

I'm thinking to myself: *Holy shit. Oh, God. Holy shit. Oh, God.*

G-mo slowly tries to reach for his bike. I can hear all the panic in his deep, gasping breaths.

"Where're you coming from?" the cop asks. "You came from robbing the store? Bunch of thugs just ran in this direction. You one of them, huh?"

My thoughts start to run a marathon, so long and far, going miles away from this city, as hot tears streak my cold face, drying beneath my nose. "No—no, we didn't rob anyone!"

The cop shows his hands, his knee in the boy's back, and clutched neatly in his fist is his gun, aimed at us.

"Hold up, hold up! What're you doing?" Tyler says.

"Hands up!" the cop shouts, foaming at the mouth from the anger inside him. The darkness kind of covers his face, but not his hatred. "Do not fucking move!"

"Ohshit," Ivy says all as one word, her arms shaking while raised. I hear a low scream.

"Oh fuck, oh fuck," G-mo goes, like he knows this is going

to be the end of the road for us. We've heard too many stories and seen too many things not to feel like this could be it for us, that it could be a white police officer signing our death certificates tonight.

A yelp emerges from the void in my gut. The air suddenly feels rough against my skin. In that moment, I replay the time when Mama got pulled over for speeding with Tyler and me in the back seat when we were eleven. "Keep your head down," she said to us. "Breathe right. Breathe easy." Mama and Dad didn't teach Tyler and me to be afraid of the cops—only to listen to their orders.

G-mo, Ivy, and I have our hands in the air like we're reaching up to touch the sky and collect all the stars. Mama taught me that listening is as important as breathing. That it can save your life. And I'm telling myself that right now is the best time for me to listen to her. Listen to this cop. Comply. Don't make a move. Keep my hands up. But Tyler doesn't.

"The fuck he gon' do," Tyler mutters as he stands up.

I jump to my feet and push Tyler behind me, stretching out my arms as if I'm a shield. "Stop moving," I say, giving him a worried look, seeing the reflection of a streetlight in his brown eyes. He pushes past me anyway.

"He ain't gon' do anything," Tyler says. "We ain't do nothing to begin with."

The cop shouts, "Don't fucking move!"

I make sure not to move. "Sir, what did we do?" I ask, trying not to sound as terrified as I really am.

The officer doesn't say anything, just breathes heavy and keeps his gun pointed at us, wanting us to move, as if waiting for us to give him a reason to shoot, a way to get away with murder.

And it's like he doesn't even notice that there's a white boy there with his face buried in the concrete sidewalk like it's a pillow.

"What happened, officer?" G-mo asks, his voice moving slow like molasses—sounding heavy like it, too. "I'm sure this is some sort of misunderstanding."

"Shut the hell up," the cop barks.

"We deserve to know. We're innocent. We're kids. And you have a gun pointed at us. What's going on?" Ivy chimes in, her voice filled with defeat.

Silence. I breathe out the air I'm holding in.

"Look, man," Tyler goes, his voice not even cracking, "you've got a fucking gun pointed at us and shit, and we just wanna know why. We were just trying to get home."

More silence.

Tyler breaks it. "A'ight, y'all need—"

"Tyler, be quiet!" I shout.

"No, he out here acting like—"

"Say one more goddamn word," the officer says, "and I'll shoot. I swear to God, I'll do it."

I look over at Tyler and see his face completely change, as if he's backpedaling in his thoughts, remembering: *Keep your head down. Breathe right. Breathe easy.*

"Don't fucking play with me," the cop yells. "I'm sick and tired of fucking responding to calls because some thugs are terrorizing the poor businesses around here. Do you even know how lucky y'all are?" he asks, his hands shaking around the butt of his gun. "How lucky y'all are to have white-owned businesses in this area? Those poor people have made sacrifices, and this is the way y'all treat them? I'm sick and tired."

"Please, officer," I mumble, my arms looking like noodles. "Please, don't shoot. Don't kill us. Please let us go!"

"Boy, I swear, I'll pull this trigger!" the officer barks. "Shut. The. Fuck. Up!" And he's not lying. His trigger finger starts shaking.

And it's in this moment that I realize that 1) the cop has definitely confused us for some other kids, 2) he is racist, and 3) we're going to die.

"Sir, we were just heading home, I swear," I say, pleading, taking huge gulps of air in between words. "We didn't...do...anything. You have...the wrong people. We were just...heading home." I try and try and try so hard to explain, but nothing, no remorse, no sympathy, no second thoughts, no step back, no removal of the gun from innocent kids' faces, absolutely fucking nothing.

My arms start to feel numb from being raised so high, so straight, so still. But I keep telling myself over and over again that if I move a single muscle in my arms, it'd be the end of me. I'm not ready to die, so I keep still even though my arms burn.

And then out of nowhere, the white kid lunges up from the ground and tackles the cop like an ass-kicking prodigy or something.

A shot is fired, but I don't see where it came from and I don't know where it landed. But I move. And that means I'm fucked one way or another. And I keep cussing myself under my breath, saying I just gave the cop a reason to shoot me, to just fucking kill me, no further questions or commands.

The skinny white boy screams, "Run!"

It takes me a minute to realize that he's talking to *us*.

And as the cop has another problem on his hands, the four of us grab our bikes and skateboard and cut out, shouting "Oh fuck" too many times for a single lifetime.

I look up at the moon as I pedal, pedal, pedal the fuck out of my bike toward home, and I force myself to believe that I'm okay, that I'm still whole.

I've never felt so terrified in my life, and stepping foot inside my house has never given me so much relief.

When I get in, Mama isn't expecting me to be crying and struggling to catch my breath, words flying out of my mouth at warp speed.

I tell her everything that happened. And she has a hard time believing me at first. Even though G-mo, Ivy, and Tyler are telling her the same story, she finds a way to say things like "What the hell?! This can't be for real!" I think it's more for her own sanity. She likes to pretend that her sons are safe in a world where they really aren't, so she tries to force oblivion.

Mama calls the local police department to file a complaint anyway, tears streaming from her eyes—like it finally sinks in that she almost lost both her sons because of a mix-up and a crooked officer.

But the lady on the other end of the landline tells Mama that she has to wait thirty days and then file a complaint in person. So Mama hangs up, cussing under her breath, a pissed look on her face that I'm too familiar with, eyes watering and everything. For the longest while, I watch her chest heave as she rests her head in her palms.

Ivy and G-mo call their mothers to pick them up and take them home, and I watch their faces as they explain in full detail what just went down—anxious looks and tears falling from their eyes.

I can't stop thinking about what happened, my thoughts trailing off into the details, replaying it all like a movie, my face getting hotter.

Two seemingly racist cops.

An unconscious black boy.

A near-death experience.

A second chance to live.

· 2 ·

It's the middle of the night, and someone's pounding on the front door.

"Police!" I hear. The pounding gets louder, faster.

I curse under my breath, my heart skipping beats, and I feel around in the darkness to turn on my nightstand lamp. I cut it on with one tug of a string.

My alarm clock blinks at me: **2:47 AM**.

"Oh my God," I whisper-yell to myself. "Three o'clock in the fucking morning."

And then I hear some movement outside my bedroom door, and I see the red and blue flashing lights illuminating everything. Tyler comes into my room, wearing a tight white tank and some basketball shorts, a black do-rag on his head.

"Don't get the door," Tyler says, sitting down on the edge of my bed. "Mama said not to open it."

Mama's wise—a bit too wise when it comes to random police visits to the house. She's become familiar with them over the years. I mean, it's routine, the way they come banging up on your door in our neighborhood for literally anything. Crackhead found dead. Some white kid from Sojo High ran away. The car outside our house has a flat tire. Some white woman down the road says she saw a suspicious black man.

And for Mama and Tyler and me, we worry more about police visits to our house than the gang-infested streets. And Mama has already started crafting a plan for how to get out of being pinched by the po-po just because of who my dad was, if that time ever comes, a time we all pray never does.

The pounding goes on for a whole ten minutes, and I end up slipping out into the hallway, taking step after tiny step, making sure I'm not breathing too hard. But Mama is already standing at the end of the hallway, arms crossed, side-eyeing Tyler and me for being hardheaded and trying to go to the door anyway. It's like we can't ever get anything past her.

She does one of her famous eye-rolls and then exhales in frustration before walking to the front.

"What y'all want?" Mama yells to the police through the door, keeping her distance. She closes her bathrobe tightly, like she feels too exposed. "Stay away from the door," Mama whispers to me.

"Ma'am, we are here to talk about an incident that happened earlier tonight. Could we come in?"

"No, I'm not dressed," she shouts back, signaling me to get back. I step away, taking slow steps, feeling some of the iron burns in the carpet underneath my bare feet since Mama can't afford an ironing board. Tyler sneaks up behind me, catching me off guard.

"Please, ma'am, put clothes on. We'd like to speak with you about what happened."

"I don't know nothing about what happened, and I got to go to work early tomorrow. Please leave! I ain't asking y'all again."

"Ma'am, two boys died tonight."

"I said leave!"

"Ma'am, please!" an officer begs, his voice deep and low.

She sighs and then looks through the peephole. She opens the door a crack, letting some of the moonlight wash inside, and then all the way, filling big empty spaces in all of the dark corners with light. They walk in and Mama flips on the light switch.

There are two cops, both of them black. One has hair; the other doesn't. They nod at Tyler and me in a friendly manner, like they come in peace. Mama closes the door behind them.

"What's this about two boys dead?" Mama's lips tremble a bit.

"On the corner of Ninth Street and Elm, two boys were shot dead. One looks to be an accident. The other appears to be in self-defense, ma'am," the officer with hair says.

"Oh my Lord. God, help us all," Mama says, shocked, holding her face. "What happened?"

"There've been several robberies and reports of vandalism in the area. Tonight there was yet another incident where we had vandals running away from an armed store owner. The vandals were vaguely described. So, once our officer responded to the call, he apparently got the wrong guys."

I swallow hard, realizing that he's talking about what happened to us.

I give a glance to Tyler, and he wears anxiety like his

do-rag, his chest heaving and his eyes bloodshot and wide—
so wide.

Mama looks back at us, concern on her face, like she's unsure if she should tell them that her sons were the ones who were wrongly accused, but we're alive.

The other cop chimes in, putting a hand on his chest. "The scene ended with an accidental shot landing in the back of an African-American male graduate of Sojo High, killing him on impact, and a self-defense shot being fired into the chest of a Caucasian male whose name we're still trying to figure out. Apparently, some others got away, unharmed, but might be suspects."

I feel a lump in my throat, and it gets so hard to breathe. My hands get clammy. I forget to blink.

Tyler takes a step backward, his chest heaving harder.

"Those kids can't be suspects," Mama says.

"Well, why's that, ma'am?" the bald officer asks.

"Because…" She trails off, glancing at Tyler and me, like she's about to tell them that we *were* those suspects who got away. "Because…they were just kids in the wrong place at the wrong time."

The officers look at each other and then back at Mama, like they think she's hiding something, but then they give her a nod.

"Well, if you get information about them or you hear anything, please don't hesitate to give us a call. Okay? You may even win a reward of some kind."

"All right." Mama sighs.

"Thank you for your time," the bald officer says, walking out the door.

"Wait," I call after them.

"Yeah? What can I help you with, son?" the bald officer asks.

"Did that cop get in trouble? Or is he hurt?"

They look at each other again. "I'm afraid some are calling for his suspension. He did his job but didn't do it carefully enough. He put innocent kids in some real danger."

"Could've killed more than just two," I say, and then they're gone.

After I hear Mama lock the door, I breathe in and out for what feels like the first time.

"Y'all don't say nothing to nobody," Mama says. "Do you understand me?"

"Yes, ma'am," we say in unison, looking each other in the eye.

She walks around us toward her room. "Tell Ivy and G-mo what I said, too."

Finally, I'm able to make it back to my room and get a

couple more hours of sleep before starting another day of my chaotic life, returning to Sojo High.

●

Two weeks ago, I wrote my dad a letter:

> Dear Dad,
>   Is today a good day for me to give up on life?
>   Is right now in this very moment a good time to cry?
>   Hey. Dad. How is it where you are?
>   I miss you.
>
>   So much love,
>   Marvin

I would kill to have him back, and this now occupies my mind as I listen to Tupac rap about his father, who was never really there.

Nine years ago today, when I was just eight years old, my dad was sent to jail for a crime he did not commit. The memories are like scars on my brain. The police pounding on the door until the door fell inward. The screaming from Mama and Tyler. The hollering in my heart. And then blackness and arms everywhere, dragging my dad out like he was a monster to be sent back to hell. I erupted inward, feeling like I was falling apart. I screamed my eight-year-old lungs out, became a disaster, and then in a flash, I was hit over the head with one of those batons that the local Sterling Point police have. "For my own good," they said.

Writing to him helps me see past it, past the shame, even past his absence sometimes. That helps me stop crying, because one thing I still remember from him—one thing I still replay in my head—is that men don't cry, and every day I try to remember that. But, man, sometimes that's just too hard to live by.

He's five hours away, in a rusty, moldy building half-way across the state, a place that exists in the shadows and mist and ash of the world called Montgomery Correctional Facility, and I haven't been able to visit him yet. Because Mama doesn't want me to see him. And on top of that, we can't even afford the trip. To Mama, the trip to Montgomery Correctional Facility is the distance of Sterling Point to, like, Russia or some shit because it's a few hours away.

He should be here with us. He didn't do what they say he did. But because he hung around the men who did, he got the same fate.

DATE: SEPTEMBER 19, 2018

TO: MARVIN D. JOHNSON (MY SON)
FROM: JAMAL P. JOHNSON
PRISON NUMBER: 2076-14-5555
MESSAGE:

Son,

Yo-yo-yo. It's Daddy.

I miss you more than the stars miss hanging in the sky after nightfall. I hope this letter finds you in a good place, my boy. I take back what I told you about not crying. Crying can free you, son. Crying can make you see past it, past the pain that hurts your growing heart.

The best time to cry is, weird enough, at nighttime—when all the lights are out, and it's dark, when no one is around to see.

I don't like it where I am—duh. Haha! Every morning I wake, I'm shocked to be here and saddened that I'm not there... with you and Moms and Ty-Ty. But they say you get used to it by your ninth year. Maybe they're right. I'll be in here for at least ten more years, and I can't wait to see your smile again, son.

I won't ever get used to the names, the words, the hitting, or the fact that they call me a bad man, a monster. I'll stain this paper with a tear, so you'll know I'm there with you, even when we can't see each other.

Keep writing to me, sonny.

Daddy loves you. Always.

Jamal D. Johnson
Montgomery Correctional
Facility
Montgomery, AL

I change into my I DIDN'T CHOOSE THE HOOD LIFE; THE HOOD LIFE CHOSE ME polo and some joggers, and I go to do my chores before it's time for school. And, man, I'm just too excited to have heard from him to cry right now, but I know I will later. At nighttime.

· 3 ·

Tyler is my somewhat troubled, somewhat gullible twin brother. We were born on June 16 (a day that broke the record as the hottest day of the year), just two minutes apart from each other—Tyler being first. It was a sticky and miserable Saturday, Mama tells us. Dad was there for Tyler's birth, but he got sick and left before it was my turn. And sometimes, I think maybe that's just a metaphor for my entire life.

There are two types of twins in the world: identical and fraternal. Tyler and I are in the middle. We look alike in the face but are not identical. I'm slim; he's not. I'm on the darker side of the spectrum; he's not as dark. I look a lot like Dwayne Wayne from my favorite show, *A Different World*, except he had a box cut and I have a low fade, but I even own a replica of Dwayne's sunglasses; Tyler does not. Tyler and I are synonyms and we go together like salt and pepper, but we're not at all the same.

Really, though, out of all the shades of black, I got one of the darkest of the family. Tyler got a medium-brown complexion, like Dad and G-mo. But everybody always says we look more like Mama. We got her long, curly eyelashes and her hair that always curls up after a shower. Only thing we got from our dad was his nose. It's a curse that we used to make fun of each other about over Thanksgiving and other holiday dinners.

Mama's 1990 Volvo station wagon smells like a blend of cigarette ash, Tyler's gym socks from intramural sports, and mildewy leather. The seats are ripped from years of wear and tear, holes coughing for oxygen in the roof. And the windows don't even roll down. All of this and then some is why Tyler and I never look forward to rides from Mama. Especially not to Sojourner Truth High School. It sucks there's no school bus that comes to our neighborhood.

The ride is about fifteen minutes long, and we're listening to a local radio station that plays a lot of R&B oldies—Mama's favorite type of music—and she's on the phone with her older sister, Auntie Nicola.

Auntie Nicola lives all the way in Indiana, where she used to be a cop before becoming a stay-at-home mom. She was about to be recruited by the FBI, too. That's how good of a cop she was in corn land. Auntie Nicola just goes to show that not every cop is bad, which can be hard to see sometimes. Mama says Auntie Nicola made enough money to quit and marry some rich black business owner, who's supporting her and her kids—she real boujee like that.

They change convos, and now they're talking about the cops around Sterling Point and what happened to Tyler, G-mo, Ivy, and me on our way home from the store. Auntie Nicola is on speakerphone, so we hear everything. "You need to have 'the talk' with them again, girl," she says.

After she clicks off the phone, Mama goes, "When y'all get home today, I'm gonna need to talk to y'all. So best get ready." And by the sound of her voice, I already know what she and Auntie Nicola are referring to. The talk is not gonna be about the Birds and the Bees. No. This talk is going to be THE talk. The talk that happens far too many times but somehow isn't enough. The talk that all decent black mothers and fathers give to their children at least once a month. The You-Live-in-a-White-Man's-World-So-Be-Careful talk.

I know she wants to have this talk now more than ever because of what happened last night.

She parks in the drop-off section and has to get out of the car to open the doors for us, since the handles on the inside are all broken, except for the driver's. "Have a blessed day, you two," she says, strangely detached. Her tone is serious, but her words are sweet.

She kisses us both on the forehead and squeezes us real tight, like she has this feeling that at any given moment we'll be taken away from her, sent into a black hole in outer space or something highly illogical like that. People don't just get sucked away from the world. Or do they?

Tyler and I rush to A-Quad, where our lockers are. They're next to each other because they're assigned in alphabetical order. Bloodred with silver scratches from decades of badass kids keying them up, brushing up against them during hard-core make-out sessions with shanks in their back pockets. The air smells like recently lit weed.

I open my THUG LIFE backpack to put in the books I need for the day, and I notice Tyler frowning hard, shoving all the wrong books into his bag.

He slams his locker shut and turns his back to me.

"Wait, Tyler," I say, catching his elbow. I pause, meeting his gaze. "You okay?"

He rolls his eyes and licks his lips, which Mama says

makes him look lik[...]

was born. "I'm a'ight [...]

In my mind, I fli[...]

tell something is on [...]

"It's about a girl, i[...]

He fake laughs, sl[...]

slips a hand in his rig[...]

There's a short p[...]

going in the hallways, [...]

"If it's about last n[...]

just the same old dead
she forces us to wri[...]
that Shakespea[...]
I know[...]
knows[...]

"It's not," he says a bit too calmly, cutting me off.

I nod and take the hint. He doesn't want to talk. And besides, I don't really know what to say to make him, so I don't press anything. Still, I can't help but feel like he's been more distant lately, and that kind of stings.

I watch him wiggle his foot.

"I'm heading to class now," he says. "I've got a quiz later. Gotta get the answers from a friend before the bell rings."

He leaves me standing there in the hallway, trying to figure things out. I look up at the ceiling for a moment, just at brown leak spots. Then I head to class, too.

●

Ms. Tanner's high-ability English class is whack as shit. We don't learn about anything worth knowing, and today's been

white people and white poems that
te on white pages. And now she tells me
e was the world's first rapper.

that's just a load of BS. Ms. Tanner probably
t, too.

Her class is one reading after another, one project after
another—pointless shit that's meant for the white kids. You
see, this school—this classroom—wasn't meant for me. It was
meant for the white folks, as Mama always reminds me. Ms.
Tanner's class is for white folks, even though it's an honors
class and we're supposed to do honors-level stuff, like learn
about culture, learn about heritage, learn about truth, learn
about the hate the world gives to people who look like me.
Brown people. Black people. Some people, no matter what,
will just hate forever.

I look back, and in the last row, Tyler is dead-ass asleep.
That means he's going to be asking me for homework help—
no, more like for the answers. And that's all right, because
all this stuff is shit I already know anyway. Shakespeare
invented iambic pentameter, and he wrote Sonnet 18 for a
man, allegedly. A past participle is a verb, typically ending
in *ed*. Ethos, pathos, and logos are the conjoined triplets of
persuasion. Blah, blah, blah.

I've become a pro at daydreaming and pretend-listening,
blocking out the white noise coming from Ms. Tanner's

mouth. And yes, sometimes it helps that I have memorized episodes of *A Different World* to replay in my drifting thoughts.

And suddenly, I hear G-mo's voice. He whispers, "Yo. She's talking to you, dude?" And then fingers poke me in the back.

I look up, wiping at my eyes. I shake my head. "YES?!" I nearly jump out of my seat, my hands clammy and warm, like a fuse just lit inside me.

"The expression *draw a blank* is an example of what, Mr. Johnson?" says an irritated Ms. Tanner.

She glares at me, and within seconds I'm having hot flashes.

"How to load a gun?" I answer her.

She stares harder, and the entire class combusts in laughter. "An idiom," she shoots back at me. The class's laughter gets louder, and I look back and see Tyler jolting awake.

I promise I'm actually sensible. I know what an idiom is. I promise. It's just—I was caught off guard and so I didn't really know *how* to answer her, and I stumbled over the words in my head.

As she turns her attention back toward the Smart Board, I float away again inside my mind, far, far away from this place.

●

Pretty much, if you're in the hood, you've got a street name. No matter what. We nobodies don't get AKAs that are threatening and dangerous, like Big Killa or Lil Death. They give us stupid names like Dawg, Fruitcup, or Squeaky if your voice is too high, or maybe straight-up Silent for extra dramatic effect.

They call G-mo, Ivy, and me Oatmeal Creme Pies. Brown on the outside, white in the middle. We've embraced the name. Oatmeal Creme Pies are delicious—by far the most delicious Little Debbie snack—so we're proudly the Oatmeal Creme Pie Squad.

After third-period trigonometry with Mrs. Bradford, I head to the cafeteria, also known as the Lion's Den. It's supposed to resemble a mall food court, but the architect did a very shitty job, and if anything it looks like an old, run-down, hole-in-the-wall food joint in a bowling alley. It has a bunch of tables tossed in, scattered throughout.

I meet up with G-mo and Ivy at our usual shabby lunch table. We're a group of high-ability geeks who love science and *A Different World* as much as life itself, sitting amid a pool of jocks, preppies, tomboys, cheerleaders, gamers, hipsters, wannabe gangsters, and, you know, just the punks who are always getting in trouble. Our world is the tiniest of them all, but that's okay, because—as I read in some book— we don't have the power to choose where we come from. We can't choose between if we come from the bottom or top or from a tiny world of poverty or not.

"I told that chick I was messing around with to fuck off," Ivy says.

G-mo's light brown eyes get wide. "Word?"

Ivy says, "I found out she was *straight*," and she puts air quotes around the word *straight*. "I told her I ain't ever putting my mouth on hers again until they make condoms for kissing. Online dating's a real bitch."

The two of them keep going back and forth, making each other laugh. It's only three of us at a table for ten. We're as diverse as any single lunch table gets. We've got G-mo, AKA a young and improved Carlos Vives, my best friend since grade school, who's from Colombia; Ivy, who's mixed and a lesbian (which I think is dope because she gets all the superfly-looking girls); and then there's me, a slender, Southern Baptist black boy—not as black as skin gets but close—and geekier than most.

G-mo and I are eating chicken quesadillas topped with lettuce and tomatoes, but they look more like extra-flattened grilled cheese sandwiches. Ivy's smart and got an actual grilled cheese and chunky tomato soup. The three of us talk about what happened last night.

"I've been checking Twitter," G-mo says. "I haven't seen anything. Like, nothing. It's pretty crazy that no one's talking about it."

"I thought about starting a Tumblr for the guy who got killed. He went here, didn't he?" Ivy asks. Ivy's not only wise beyond her age but also really caring. I love that about her.

"That's what I heard," I reply. "It's scary and sad as shit." All my life I've heard about people getting killed by police, but I never really prepared myself for it to happen so close to my neighborhood. I mean, I figure if I stay out of trouble, and if I convince Ivy and G-mo and Tyler to do the same, and if I always do as I'm told by the law, I'll be okay.

Security guards stand around the perimeter of the cafeteria because lunch is the place where most of the fights happen. We've yet to go a single week in our school's history without a fight. Out of all the schools in all the counties within a twenty-mile radius of Sojo High, our school is known to have the most expulsions. Most of which come from fights. And since our sports teams aren't that good, we pride ourselves on being recognized for something, even if it is the highest number of physical altercations.

I turn around and catch a look at Tyler sitting with Johntae's crew, laughing and cracking jokes with one another. Tyler's never sat with Johntae and his crew before. He stopped sitting with us to sit with the jocks last year. Why the hell is he sitting *there* now? Johntae is a notorious drug dealer in Sterling Point, a Sojo High bully, a gang member, and yep— he's known to love weed like Kanye loves Kanye, or like G-mo loves masturbating. Defying all odds, Johntae has managed to stay in school, hanging on to a 1.9 GPA by paying geeks like me to do the work for him.

He's midsentence when he looks over at me, stopping his conversation with Tyler, who's sitting directly across from him. I get the feeling that Tyler's purposely not turning around, purposely not trying to catch me watching him. Johntae gives me the coldest look, and I find my eyes quickly shooting away, back to my tray.

"You know what I hate?" I ask.

"Yo. Mrs. Bradford? Don't we all," G-mo shouts a little too loudly.

"No, no," I say, sighing. "I hate how I feel trapped. I feel, like, boxed in. I feel like I'm the mouse from *Flowers for Algernon*, like I'm destined to be this geeky black boy with no sense of direction for the rest of my life. Man, I wanna live. Man, I just wanna be like them sometimes. I wanna fit in. I hate not fitting the part." And then my eyes wander back over to Johntae and his posse.

"Those guys?" G-mo goes. "Wangsters? You want to be a wangster? Who are you and what have you done with my best friend, Marvin Darren Johnson? Because the Marvin *I* know would never think about being one of them. Do you not remember that we almost lost our lives because we were mistaken for some of *them*? Fuck that."

"I don't want to be a gangster," I say. "I just want to…fit in with them. You know?"

"I get you," Ivy replies, and it's kind of nice, because Ivy is also always the understanding one. She just gets things, gets my way of thinking, like she's the girl doppelganger of me. "It'd be nice to fit in with the cheerleaders."

"You look like one," G-mo mutters to her.

"Yeah?" she asks. "My chest is so flat, though. I hear that's what the coaches look for."

"That's why you gotta get in there and bribe the shit out of the coaches. That's what a lot of them did," he says. "Like, one girl brought in blackberry pie."

"Only white people make that shit," Ivy says. We laugh.

Before I can say anything else, it happens. The fight. Today's fight ends up being between two girls. One black, big, and mean girl wearing a short skirt against another black, tomboyish-looking girl. They go at it hard, flinging weave everywhere, slapping each other with lunch trays, and then the fight makes its way over to us. One of the girls slams the other right on top of our table, the wind of the motion blowing in my face, and from here, everything sounds like crunches and bones breaking.

G-mo, Ivy, and I jump back from the table, and then security and Principal Dodson run over to stop the girls from ripping each other's heads off. After they go, all that's left around us is a lingering waft of sweat and musty armpit and hair grease.

●

Later, after fifth period, I get called into Principal Dodson's office. The tiny room is filled with coffee stains and spilled mustard trails and stacks of old papers and books, and it takes only a couple seconds for me to break into a sweat, beads falling into my eyes. The office smells and is as hot as the devil's ass crack, and it makes me literally itch all over, to the point where I have to make a mental note to shower ASAP.

Principal Dodson looks like a fifty-year-old ex–football player: broad shoulders, a mean expression always on his face, a line of sweat running down his black forehead like he's coming from the gym. Most of the teachers here are white, and I used to think Dodson and I would get along because of our shared culture. Nope. One time, he wore icicle-shaped cuff links just to prove he's made of ice. He has a reputation of being a dick, so most try to avoid him.

"Mr. Johnson," he says. "Do you know why you're in my office?"

"No, sir." My hands get a little clammy and sweat coats

my palms thickly, like my hands got dipped in jars of Vaseline, so I wipe them off on my pants.

And then Dodson leans back in his desk chair, waving a packet in my face. "You know what this is?"

"No, sir," I answer, unable to read what's on the pages.

"Look closer." He tosses me the papers.

It's the paper I recently turned in for my English class. The one about my favorite show, *A Different World*.

"Why should I give my time to someone like you, who doesn't really give a damn?" Dodson yells at me from across his cluttered desk, books and piles of paper covering the surface. His voice is loud and piercing, stabbing my ears.

"But I put a lot of thought into that paper. The assignment was to write about a piece of art I find inspiring. Dwayne Wayne is my hero, and this show actually paints my reality."

Dodson just laughs in my face, like what I've told him is the funniest thing he's heard in a while. A tear even rolls down his cheek—that's how hard he laughs. And then when his laughter winds down, he glares at me in silence, waiting for me to take back my words. I stare at him, too. My hands get moist, and sweat beads my palms again.

"So, you really think some TV show counts as art?" Anger gleams in his eyes, like days of rage that have been building up are about to be unleashed on me.

"*A Different World* was—is—more than just…some *TV show*," I shoot back at him, as confident as ever, pressing my fingers into his desk to emphasize my words. "*A Different World* shows blackness in a way not many other shows do. It taught me that I could be successful, even when people think otherwise. It taught me not to be afraid of daring to be different. The characters knew what it meant to be like me."

Dodson laughs sarcastically. "So, a TV show taught you that, but not important writers like Langston Hughes and Toni Morrison?"

"Sir, that's not what I'm saying," I mutter, shrugging my shoulders. "Not to be rude or anything, but black people aren't a monolith, and we're allowed to be inspired by more than one thing or a handful of people. Hughes is my favorite poet, but that doesn't mean he's the only person who inspires me."

"That's the most ridiculous thing I've ever heard. Wait, no—your paper is definitely more ridiculous."

My heart sinks in my chest. And I remember what Dad wrote in his letter. It's best to cry when it's dark and I'm alone. So right now isn't the time to cry, even though I feel like just busting out in a watery stream.

"You really have the audacity to think that MIT's gonna accept somebody who doesn't take school seriously? I'm going to be real clear with you. Unless you're going to start treating your education with respect, you might as well keep MIT out of your vocabulary."

"What?"

"This is real life, not the movies. Boys like you don't have a place at MIT. Or any of the prestigious schools in America."

"Well, Mr. Dodson, sir, I'd like to think otherwise. I think there's plenty of room for boys who look like me. But people like you make it hard for us to see that."

"Who do you think you are?" he bellows, getting out of his chair, leaning in toward me. "You go to Sojo Truth High School, one of the worst-rated schools in the state. To the admissions committee, your high-ability classes, your straight As, your *inspiration*—none of that means shit."

"But…sir…" And suddenly, I just want to scream at the top of my fucking lungs, because right now I'm reminded that I'm not enough, never ever will be enough. That I will never get out of here. *A Different World* is just fiction. There's no future for people like me.

He rolls his eyes and balls up a fist, almost gnawing on it 'cause he's on edge.

"Get out of my office and get to class" is all he says.

I exhale deeply before grabbing my backpack and my paper and walking toward his office door. Just when I touch the doorknob, it creaks, and his ceiling fan wheezes. I look back at him and see his eyes still glued to me.

I tell him, "Oh, and by the way, if you ever get a chance, you should watch an episode. It'll show you what education has the potential to be. You might even like it."

And I leave his office.

· 4 ·

In the hallway, as I head back to class, I run into Johntae and Tyler shaking it up like they're longtime friends or something. The hallways are normally tight and crowded as shit, the stench itching my nostrils, but right now they're empty. And out of all the possible combinations in all of Sojo Truth High, my brother and Johntae are the only two standing in front of the science lab, slapping hands and smiling at each other. What could Tyler possibly be doing with somebody like Johntae?

I clear my throat loud enough to interrupt this fuckery going on.

And shit gets hella awkward.

Tyler looks at me. He stands there in his Sojo Truth High sports hoodie and jeans. He nods with a forced smile. The way he looks at me tells me he's hiding something. The look on his face shows he's becoming someone else. And for a split second, I'm thinking, *Maybe this is how Cain looked at Abel?*

"What up, bro?" he says.

"Nothing, nothing much, just...uh...coolin'."

He chuckles before walking down the hallway to his next class, his backpack, unzipped, dangling on his left shoulder. "Catch you later, then, bro! Oh, and remind Ma that I'll be home a little late—I'm hanging with some dudes." He gives me that warm brotherly smile.

"All right." I wave at him until he's completely out of sight.

And it hits me that I am all damn alone in the hallway with Johntae. Even if he and my bro are suddenly tight or whatever, he could still give me shit.

He blinks real long and hard. "Well, well, well, if it isn't Marvin the tree monkey," he grunts. A whack-ass line to scare me, but it works. There's a lump in my throat, and my mind runs through all the possibilities of what's about to go down. Around other people, Johntae does only minor things to me, like shove me into my locker and knock my books out of my hands, Karate Kid–style—but now we aren't around other people. I blink, flinching hard, my heart racing.

Johntae's a legit thug who dresses like the stereotype of one. Black do-rag. Bandana. Black T-shirt so long that it passes his knees. Baggy jeans. White kicks, untied and polished.

He steps closer until we're only inches away from each other. "I swear you and your geeky friends are some little Creme Pies, always acting all gooey and white," he bellows, holding his pants up with one hand, the other pointing in my face.

"Well…maybe you need to reconsider your definition of what it means to be black." I struggle to speak, the words feeling almost physically painful as they fall from my tongue. "Being black doesn't just mean repping the hood, right?"

Johntae laughs an unexpected laugh. It's a booming one, like an overly amused hyena, with a little hood in it—like you can hear his hard life in between the *ha*s. He gets even closer, until I can actually feel him breathing on my face. "Blood, you don't know nothing about the hood. You don't get that experience until you're shot and stabbed in the back from being out there on the streets selling dope to get by, you hear?"

I gulp, swallowing down a knot, and nod like his words are death sentences.

And then he steps away and scans me up and down, his eyes stopping for a bit too long at my chain. It was my dad's chain, and it's one of the only pieces of him I still have. Shit. I feel the world narrowing and closing in.

"Hot daaaamn," he says lowly, his fist pressed to his mouth. He pauses for a short moment, looking into my eyes, and then continues. "Oh yeah, you gonna have to give me that."

"What?"

"You heard me, lil nigga. Give me your chain."

"It's worthless," I lie to him.

He cocks his head up and bites his lip. "I don't give a shit." He launches his body at me and slams me against the wall of metal lockers, cold against cold. My head hits hard enough for a concussion, and my vision blurs for a moment. He grips my collar tightly in his hands, his fingernails cutting into my neck. As I wheeze and gasp, my head feeling like it'll explode, he says with a sneer, "I'm not gonna repeat myself."

I nod, my eyes slowly closing from the pressure.

Then I'm released. My skull doesn't feel like it's slowly breaking into tiny pieces anymore. And I have a grip on my vision again.

Slowly but surely, I pull the chain up from around my neck and drop it into his open palm.

"Why me?"

"You ain't like me," he says. "That's why."

"What?"

"You different," Johntae says before waddling down the hallway toward C-Quad, his pants nearly tripping him at his ashy ankles. And he chucks me the bird, muttering, "Pussy-ass bitch."

Man, ain't this some fucked-up shit.

●

Just when I get ready to head home, I look both ways and see Tyler in the distance.

He's standing around with Johntae and his crew, pants sagging lower than usual, wearing his gray sports hoodie and a snapback. *I don't understand how, even when it's been so long since he's played sports, Tyler still manages to wear that hoodie.*

Tyler looks at something in his hand as Johntae talks to him, poking him in the chest. It's like he's in trouble, big trouble for some shit. And my heart is beating so hard.

Tyler pulls out a folded baggie and slips it into his other palm, closing it tightly, and then he eases it over to Johntae. It's all shady as hell.

Johntae smiles, nodding in appreciation.

Tyler nods back, but in fear. My heart thuds in triplets now.

And then I catch Johntae slip Tyler a wad of cash.

God, please, no.

I stand there, just watching Tyler talk and laugh with Johntae. But instead of waiting for my nuts to drop and rescuing Tyler, I end up walking home, taking a shortcut through a series of backyards, climbing fences, and cutting through gated communities.

· 5 ·

I look around me, taking in everything I see, until I start to breathe this neighborhood, exhaling it, knowing it through and through. Little girls playing hopscotch written in multi-colored chalk on the sidewalks. Older boys playing football on opposite sides of the cracked street, dividing them even more, degrees of separation between them. Parents sitting in lawn chairs on their porches, sipping cheap coolers. Fake smiles. Fake nods. Fake happiness.

When I walk into my room, I see that G-mo's already made himself a ham sandwich and Ivy's lying across the foot of my bed, flipping through a *Game Informer* magazine, her phone blaring "Hip Hop Ride" by Da Youngstas as loud as it can.

"Did you know there's a new Call of Duty game coming out?"

G-mo's eyes get wide and he lunges up from the floor to look at the magazine.

I shake my head and shrug. "Those games would be so much better with less CGI. I always get nauseous playing."

"They need *more* CGI. I need to see more blood and guts," G-mo says back through a mouthful of sandwich.

"It's hot as balls in here." I can feel the sweat already forming on my forehead.

I sit my backpack in the corner of the room and crack open my window since we don't have A/C. The bill doubled this month, and Mama doesn't make enough to pay it. Besides, there's a nice, steady breeze out right now.

"I saw something and I don't know what to do," I say.

Ivy turns off the music and eases up off the bed a bit, giving me a concerned look.

"What?" G-mo whisper-yells. "Mr. and Mrs. Hornberg were having sex in the gym again? If so, you kind of have to expect that at this point. I mean, yo, look at their last name."

"No. I think Tyler's a drug dealer."

"What the fuck? Like, for real?" Ivy goes, her nostrils widening.

"When he was with Johntae and his crew, I saw them exchange some package. I swear it was drugs or something."

"Dude. What're you going to do?" G-mo asks.

"I—"

There's a knock on my bedroom door, which is cracked open. It's Tyler.

"Hey, bro," he says with this desperate look on his face, his do-rag still on. I didn't realize he'd started wearing it during the day, so it catches me off guard for a moment.

I blink back my focus on him. "Hey."

"You seen my ham? I don't see it in the fridge. I hid the last piece so no one would eat it."

Ivy snorts and covers her face with the *Game Informer*. I look back at G-mo, whose face goes from *This sandwich is bomb* to *I'm fucked*, and I roll my eyes before turning back to Tyler.

"Mama told you about hiding food," I say, looking up at his fivehead.

"Yeah, but you know every time Mama buys something sweet, she's always hiding it in her room, too. Soda, candy, the whole nine yards."

I have a two-second crisis with myself on what to say back now. G-mo's looking at me, pleading with his eyes, but I can't lie to Tyler.

"G-mo ate it," I admit, and a laugh slips out.

"Fuck you, Marvin! I thought we were never-snitch homies, like Harry and Ron," G-mo shouts, jumping to his feet, swallowing the last piece of sandwich as if to destroy all evidence. "Look, Tyler, I promise, bro, I didn't know it was yours. I had this really disgusting-looking whatever-the-fuck-it-was for lunch and I—"

"It's cool," Tyler interrupts him, and smiles. "It's cool. I'll get some from the store next time I go."

Not sure where this sudden burst of kindness comes from, but I like it. This is the Tyler Johnson I know and love. Suddenly, I'm remembering when we were in elementary school, when we lived on the South Side and had to share a bedroom. Some nights, after Mama made sure all the lights were out and our eyes were shut, and Tyler and I knew Mama was in a deep sleep, we would sneak out the window to shoot some hoops with the court set we'd gotten the previous Christmas. One night, I played barefoot, and after a jump shot, I came down on a smashed beer bottle. I couldn't see much, but I could feel wetness everywhere. After Tyler and I snuck back in, he cleaned out the cut with alcohol and peroxide, bandaged it, and helped me back into bed. I limped for a whole week, and every time Mama noticed she would say, "Boy, what the hell wrong with your foot?" Tyler said we were messing around and he accidentally stepped on it.

I breathe in and ask Tyler if he wants to go play ball later tonight.

He hesitates. "Not tonight—I'm busy. Another time, though, all right?"

Busy? What kind of busy? I can feel my throat drying, my eyes growing wider by the second, and it's getting harder to shrug off my thoughts.

Before I can even ask him, just to reassure myself that it's not what I think it is, that he's dealing drugs or whatever, he stops me. "Oh yeah, Johntae is having this party on Friday and he said I could invite whoever I wanted. I want you three there. It'll be lots of girls there. I'm tellin' you, it's about to be so damn lit."

Ivy and G-mo shout, speaking over each other. "Holy shit? Us? Johntae's party? Girls? We are in."

My heart picks up its pace. Tyler's standing there, grinning in my face, like he's not best friends with the neighborhood drug dealer and everything's fine, and it takes everything for me not to punch some sense into him. And Ivy and G-mo are behind me acting like some invisible person is twerking on them, shouting how we are going to get laid.

"No, we're not going," I say, interrupting their moment. Tyler's smile wipes clean off his face, and he gives me this hurt look.

"WHAT?!" G-mo and Ivy say in unison, like it's the

single most bonkers thing they've heard in their entire lives. Like accepting a drug dealer's invite to a party is the same as accepting an invitation to Beyoncé and JAY-Z's wedding. Like it's a fucking honor.

Then, Ivy adds, "Dude, why the fuck not? We're going. We need to meet some girls." She pauses. "Weekends are for parties and meeting girls."

I blink.

My weekends normally consist of waking up, eating breakfast, doing chores, writing letters to Dad, reading letters from Dad, filtering through our old letters, more chores (because those are never done, according to Mama), getting ahead with homework, looking up photos of Megan Fox and Zoe Saldana, and unashamedly masturbating. But still. Johntae's party isn't worth the risk of ruining my chances of getting into MIT, if something were to happen.

"Fuck Johntae. Fuck his party. I don't care."

"Yo! You are legit tripping right now."

"Why won't you come, Marvin?" Tyler asks, still looking hurt. "Quit acting like that."

I don't turn around to look at G-mo and Ivy, but I hear all of their annoying pleading.

"I'm not going to a fucking drug dealer's party, Tyler! One, Mama would beat the black off me if she found out, and two, nothing good can come from going." I turn to G-mo and Ivy.

"But if that's what you two want to do, go the fuck ahead!" I throw my hands up.

Tyler walks closer to me, and he gets so close I can feel his breath on my face. He clamps his hands down on my shoulders. "Look, Marvin, it's not easy without Dad around, and Mama can't support us on her own. You see her struggling. Can't pay the bills, let alone send you to college. Johntae's going to help with that. So that's all this is."

"I call bullshit, Tyler."

He exhales deeply with frustration, rolling his eyes. "You're just like Ma. So negative. You know, you're both like prison wardens."

"What? Tyler, sound it the hell out. These. Are. Gangsters."

There's a pause. I can hear my heartbeat in my ears. I look back at Ivy and G-mo, and they're glancing down, chins in hand, as if they're soaking in the moment.

"I'm having Johntae text our phone the address. Show up, if you change your mind. All of you."

There's another pause as an electric volt shoots through my body, and a huge sigh slips out.

Tyler walks away, readjusting his do-rag. I stand in the same place until I hear him walk out the front door.

· 6 ·

Mama used to say, "Families that eat together stay together." But Dad's not here. Tyler's not here. It's just her and me at this silent table, looking at each other and eating spaghetti grilled cheeses made with leftover spaghetti. (I'm not complaining. It was either this or cabbage-water soup.) But after Mama questions me about Tyler's whereabouts for the second time, and after I lie that he's staying late to study for the SAT with friends, he shows up.

His shirt is torn and his backpack is covered in mud. He smells funky, like recently lit weed and armpit.

"Where've you been?" A frantic look forms on Mama's face. "You late."

Tyler's eyes fall to the floor, and he scratches the back of his neck, his backpack falling off him a bit. "Studying," he lies. I don't even know why he bothers lying. Mama is like a living, breathing lie detector.

Mama folds her arms in her seat. "Studying, huh?"

Tyler just nods. Still scratching away.

And this shabby little house of ours gets twenty degrees hotter all in a matter of seconds. I can see his eye twitch. I bet Mama can, too.

"Who was you with?" she asks.

Tyler tosses his backpack back over his shoulder, and his voice gets all low and apologetic. "The guys."

"The. Guys?" She punctuates her words, slow and jabbing. This is about to be ugly. I can feel it in my queasy gut. "What're their names? Where do they live? And why don't I know them?" Her voice gets louder and shakier.

Tyler pauses for a bit, his eyes blinking fast. He barely gets the names out, stumbling over the syllables, like rocks on the sidewalk. "Johntae, Fish, Zig, Big Money, and Moe."

She gets out of her chair and slaps him hard against the side of his face with a popping sound. "What the hell kind of name is Big Money and Fish? What're their real names?"

Tyler just shrugs his broad shoulders and scrunches up

his mouth, confused. His scratching moves to his nose. "I don't know."

"You don't know?"

"I just call them what they want to be called," Tyler answers.

"You know what's about to be calling you? This belt," Mama shouts, pointing a finger into Tyler's chest. But instead of pulling off her belt for real and waling on Tyler, she closes her eyes tightly, breathes in, cocks her head back, and then walks over to the table and pulls up a seat, shaking her head.

Then, she opens her eyes as wide as ever, pulling out a cigarette and lighting it in between her fingers. "I just want y'all boys to be safe out here. That's all I ask: Do your chores, get good grades, and be safe. There's too much going on in the world. Folks done lost they minds, snatching up kids and killing everybody. I just couldn't imagine what I would do if something were to happen to one of you."

I look over at Tyler, and his face actually looks remorseful. "I'm sorry, Mama," Tyler says, and even I fall for it.

"All right now," she accepts, and points to the stove. "I made dinner. It might be cold, but a microwave's over there."

She puffs out an almost perfect cloud of smoke. If there's one thing I've learned since she brought me into this world, it's that you'll never quite understand her. It's like Mama's cigarettes are the only things that wholly get her.

I walk by Tyler's room. He's sitting on the edge of his twin-sized bed, his eyes cold, brown, and drained, like coffee stains. He gives me one slow nod, and I walk inside and sit next to him on the bed, looking around like I've just stepped inside Mr. Magorium's Wonder Emporium. His hideout is a graffiti mural plastered in posters and sports cards.

"I'm never lying for you again, Tyler. You gotta stop hanging with Johntae and them. Please. For Mama and me. You heard what she said."

He inches away a bit, his sheets rustling, and he finally says, "It ain't that simple."

"Look, I just want to talk." I stare straight ahead, my hands folded in my lap.

"There's nothing to talk about."

Up close, I can see the dark circles underneath his eyes. And I can't believe it, but Tyler is actually crying, and he's giving it his all to hide it from me. But it's a losing battle.

We sit in silence for a couple moments. I'm not sure what Tyler's thinking, but I know the only thing running through my mind is the fact that my own brother is straying away from me, and this is just my desperate attempt at calling him back.

"Remember all those mixtapes you made?" I ask.

He laughs with watery eyes. "Yeah. They're somewhere in here. In a box or drawer, buried, never to be heard by another human being."

"No, man, you were actually good at beats. It used to be all that you'd listen to, remember?"

"Of course I remember! That's when I thought I was the shit. I actually thought I could sell tapes and make it the way Biggie did. Still do, sometimes. FruityLoops and that illegal version of GarageBand I had helped me get through middle school and freshman year."

"Mm-hmm, you were a bad middle school student," I joke.

"Those were some rough years, and my beats were the only thing that kept me going. I had this fire in me that if I powered through, I could be, like, the next Dr. Dre or something." He lets out a small laugh. "Those mixtapes were a perfect distraction from everything."

He nudges me in the arm, and I look up at him as he flashes me a small grin. Then I look away.

It goes quiet. I breathe in deeply, and the strong and lingering stench of weed fills up my nostrils.

"You stink," I say. "You should take a shower."

He buries his head in his armpit; he takes a huge whiff and then smells his sleeves. "Dammit! I didn't think it would be this bad."

We lift off the bed simultaneously. "So, you smoke now?" I shoot him a disappointed look, furrowing my eyebrows.

Tyler rolls his eyes. "No. The guys did, though."

He rips off his shirt and throws it across the room, into the hamper by his cracked and peeling wooden dresser. He puts on a tight black tank top, squeezing into it.

Out of nowhere, I blurt, "I don't want to lose you to them, Tyler."

He looks surprised—his eyebrows caving in, lines forming on his forehead.

"You won't. I'll always be here. For you and Mama." He rubs his eyes. "No one will ever take me away from you two."

It goes quiet again. The world feels like it speeds up.

"I'm sorry." His voice is the quietest it's been since I came in here. "I shouldn't have said those shitty things to you earlier."

"It's okay," I say, and he gives me dap, like he used to. "Ty, I know you think you need to be hanging out with Johntae and dudes like him to fulfill some sort of prophecy the world predicts for you—or for us—but trust me when I say there are better ways."

I watch him search his drawers for a change of clothes, and he tosses a clean pair of cheap boxers over his shoulder before he responds.

"Like I said: No one's taking me away."

I bite my lip and turn back.

"Hey, Marvin, one other thing." We look at each other a final time. "I don't say it a lot, but I love you, bro."

I force a small smile at him before heading to my room. For the first time in a while, the air I breathe in, and everything else, is just...peaceful.

· 7 ·

Even though my stomach turns sour every time the thought of Johntae's party enters my mind, I text Ivy and G-mo that the only reason I'm going is to play Spy on My Twin. None of us has an actual driver's license, so we meet up at my place and pedal our way under the still, blue sky to some mystery location that Johntae sent Tyler in a text and my nuts get really sore and tender riding on my bike, the seat worn all the way down to the metal frame.

Two numb nuts and a handful of minutes later, I arrive with G-mo and Ivy to this brick warehouse—looking building that used to be a flea market. I believe they called it Pic-A-Rag or something. Yeah, that's it. A trash market owned by an old friend of Mama's that got closed down because of roaches and too many robberies. For the longest time, I thought this building was abandoned, never to be used again—or maybe a place for all the homeless people of Sterling Point to take up permanent residence. But it looks totally redone from the outside, and I can only imagine what the inside is like. I guess drug dealers can afford this kind of renovation.

The line to get in is strangely long, like all of Sojo Truth High School was invited and they just so happened to bring everybody and their mama. There's a bouncer and a slew of security guards standing on both sides of the red carpet and cutoff line rope.

And I'm all like, "What kind of drug dealer gets security guards and a bouncer at a party?" More important, though, what kind of security guards and bouncers agree to work a drug dealer's party—a drug dealer's *anything*?

"Does it really matter?" G-mo says, slapping his dry hands together like he's about to get some grub. He twists his marijuana-green hat, turning it backward to look more suave than he really is.

"Yeah, who cares? All I want is to find me a fine-ass honey," Ivy says, her eyes all dolled up with gold eyeliner. She's also wearing skinny disco pants—black ones, with a white tank top and a blue jean jacket. I'm in my Notorious B.I.G. hoodie and some black jeans. The three of us really could be our own pop group or something.

G-mo and Ivy shake up hands, like they've made a bro pact or something—that they both have to leave this party 1) with a girl and 2) without their virginity.

My fists clutch at my sides, and I find myself sighing a bit too loudly, looking around, and checking the long line over and over again, seeing it grow.

"What's up with you?" Ivy says, putting her hand on my shoulder. "You seem...tense."

"Nothing," G-mo answers for me. "He just desperately needs to get laid." And he laughs at his own joke, like it's the greatest thing ever, but even Ivy doesn't laugh.

Out the corner of my eye, I see Tyler entering a side door with a couple other guys who belong to Johntae's crew. The angst is all over my body now, like goose bumps. I remain fixed on him as the anxiety pinches at the back of my throat. I'm afraid to see something I don't really want to see. I'm afraid of knowing the truth.

Images flash through my mind of the time I saw Tyler with Johntae, dealing in the middle of the day, at Sojo High. One image haunts me: Tyler ending up like Dad—in jail, just plucked from my life.

I'm stuck in this slippery gray area between grieving the absence of my dad and watching my brother slowly vanish before my eyes. My knuckles crack as I squeeze them together. I got to remind myself to lay low and keep an eye on Tyler.

"You worry about him a lot," Ivy says.

"Yeah." I nod. "I worry like hell."

She rolls up her sleeves and puts both her hands on my arms, standing in front of me to block my view of the entrance. "Worrying is stupid—but, man, it shows you've got a big heart in your chest. Your brother's lucky to have you, M. You always got his back."

I smile, and she lets me go.

I look up at the sky, and something tells me that things just might be okay.

•

The inside is everything I expect it to be and more. We walk through a long hallway, like a tunnel, to get the main floor. Different-colored strobe lights line the ceiling. Loud music. People dancing—no, grinding on each other. The smell of sweat and lit weed weaving through the air.

There's a girl walking toward me. She's tall and showing her natural hair in an Afro. Her cheetah-print shirt, the matching bottoms, the glitter around her eyes. She's fine as hell. When she's closer, I see she's wearing a necklace that spells out *Faith*.

She brushes up against me, giving me chills. And I'm just left staring at her, pressing every inch of her into my thoughts.

She winks at me, and I feel like I'm going to die of the world's biggest, hardest erection, but I have to remind myself why I'm really here.

Not for girls. Not for girls.

I place my hands in front of my junk and watch as she passes by, the world feeling like it's rotating slower and slower.

"My. Gay. God," Ivy says, watching this girl in a shiny, sparkly dress flip her hair.

I catch G-mo turning his head to the side, scanning her up and down. I punch his arm and he tosses his hands in the air, like he's surrendering.

Something makes me look behind me, and my eyes zoom into focus on a scene that completely kills all the fluttering feelings in my stomach.

And at the end of the hallway, Johntae has Tyler pinned to the wall. His crew members just watch, like they're getting off on watching my brother's pain. Tyler chokes, trying hard to catch his breath and push his weight off the wall.

I run toward them, screaming and hollering for him to let Tyler go. "Fucking let him go, I said!" My voice cracks as I yell, the veins in my head throbbing.

When Johntae catches sight of me, he releases Tyler at once. Gravity pulls Tyler's body down hard to the floor, and he gasps heavily, taking in huge gulps of oxygen, his own hands wrapped tightly around his throat.

"What's up, lil homie?" Johntae nods at me, like he didn't just have my brother in a chokehold against the wall. He goes in to shake up with me, but I brush past him, bending down to check on Tyler.

"Tyler? Are you all right?"

He shakes his head fast and spits on the floor. "I'm fine, I'm fine. Get off me!" He rises from the floor, using the wall to keep his balance. A familiar emptiness and darkness in his eyes.

I step back some more. Tyler and Johntae stare at each other in silence, like they're about to fight cowboy-style— like those old Western movies Mama used to watch, with the tumbleweeds rolling in the desert.

"I'm sick and tired of the games," Johntae says to Tyler.

"What games?" Tyler says.

"You know what the fuck I mean. I put loyalty above everything. Don't fuck with me again."

I can tell my brother's scared, that he's nervous, but he's

pretending to be hard. "For the hundredth time," Tyler says, biting his lip and clenching his fists, "it was *not* me, man. I ain't a snitch."

"Just know that you're already in my hand. The only thing I haven't done yet is close my fist."

Tyler looks at me and then at Johntae and then walks away into the huge grinding crowd, everyone dancing to a song by Drake.

"Go on in and enjoy all this party has to offer you, lil homie," Johntae says, blowing his blunted breath all over me, a huge grin stuck on his face, like he and I are estranged cousins.

I push past him, Ivy and G waiting nearby. We walk through the crowd, the three of us. All the people here are like goldfish swimming around in electrically charged water in a giant fishbowl, brushing up against one another with each move as the song switches to some new track by A$AP Rocky.

Tyler is nowhere to be found.

I push through a few sweaty bodies. The floor has a long green carpet littered with ash, empty alcohol bottles, and red Solo cups. There're screams echoing toward us, coming from the back. It kind of feels like a mini earthquake within these weed-tainted walls, people's feet shuffling and sneakers squeaking. My stomach flips over and over, and it gets so loud.

I freeze in place, trying to find my way through the stampede of people running toward me. The strobe lights are cut, everything goes dark, and then the emergency lights and sirens blare to life.

Ivy grabs my arm. G-mo grabs on to her. We try to stay together.

And then gunshots are fired.

Pow! Pow! Pop!

Screaming. Screaming. SCREAMING. *Man, what the fuck is happening?*

I grab for Ivy's hand and pull her to my side, pressing our bodies down as we duck and crawl to safety. A few more shots ring out, and my instinct is to freak the fuck out. I shouldn't have come here.

Everything spins and blurs, and it feels like I'm going to faint as people run past me toward the exit doors, screaming.

"I gotta make sure Tyler is okay," I shout over all the screams.

Ivy and G-mo yell at me not to go, but I have to make sure he's okay. I squeeze through many sweaty bodies, tripping over debris, ducking and hoping I'm not in the way of bullets. My heart is about to give out and I can't breathe. I don't see him. I don't see him anywhere. I turn around to head back to Ivy and G-mo so we can get the hell out of this place, thinking, *Maybe Tyler got out safely. Maybe he's already outside.*

Pow! Pop! This is what I hear. Then, a crash.

Pow! Pop!

The battlefield that was once *inside* me upon stepping into this place is actually becoming real. I run and shield myself behind a fallen table. In my head, I'm imagining I'm six all over again, hearing my first drive-by.

I crawl away from the dance floor. When I get to safety, G-mo and Ivy are there to help me up. We get outside. I gasp for fresh air, searching the crowd for Tyler.

I don't see him anywhere. *Shit, Tyler, where are you?*

The loud sirens of police and then more screaming and rounds of bullets block my thoughts. And we run to our bikes, cutting through the back woods to get to my place.

●

At home, Tyler is nowhere to be found. G-mo, Ivy, and I check the kitchen, the living room, every bedroom, even the bathroom. Mama's not home either, but I pull out the phone I share with Tyler and realize she called me a shit-ton of times and sent me a bunch of texts saying that she was going out for drinks with some new friend of hers and just reminding Tyler and me to be safe and that she loves us. I think she's dating again.

And it finally hits me. I can't even call him because I have our phone. I try to call Johntae. He doesn't answer. My heart has pounded its way numb—everything feels like I'm being closed in, and my skin burns like the moment I saw the look in Tyler's eyes when he last walked away from me. The emptiness. I want to scream.

"Shit, shit, shit!" I yell, walking back and forth in the living room.

G-mo and Ivy are waiting on the couch for their parents with horrified looks on their faces, both on the verge of tears.

"What the actual fuck?" G-mo repeats on loop, holding his arms together as if to make sure he's still in one piece.

I pause in place, taking a deep breath for what feels like the first time. My entire body is shaking, a chill shooting through me. I turn back to look at the front door. "Where are you, Tyler?" I wait for him to barge through at any moment.

Ivy gets to her feet, rolling up the bottoms of her pants. And with so much shock in her eyes, she says, "He's fine. He probably just left the party after Johntae treated him like shit."

G-mo keeps his bushy eyebrows raised. "What the fuck."

I gasp. And I gasp, and tears are coming out again because my thoughts are just too damn much right now. And I don't even bother to be ashamed. I don't even turn away from Ivy and G-mo.

My phone buzzes against my thigh. I snatch it from my pocket to see if it's Tyler, hoping he's somewhere safe with a working phone.

But it's not. It's Mama.

I don't even know if I should answer.

She hangs up before I give in.

Eventually, G-mo's and Ivy's parent pick them up from my place, leaving me to pace the living room, not sure of what to do. *What should I do?*

When Mama gets back home, she's still wearing her teal Tweety Bird scrubs, a pink headband on. I can tell she's had a few shots of Hennessy. I know the look when I see it.

"Where's your brother?" she asks, placing her purse on the kitchen table.

I don't know. I can't tell her that. But I can lie.

"He stayed over at a friend's place."

"What friend?" She looks up at me, squinting. "Don't you lie to me either!"

I have to look away. "Someone from school. They had a project or something. He said he'll be back by morning." Even *I* almost believe it.

Her fists clench, but all her other muscles loosen and she's breathing normally again, not wheezing with frustration, like she normally does right before she lights a cigarette.

"Does he at least have ya'll's phone?"

"No. I do."

She cuts me a side-eye so hard. "Ya'll ain't got the sense God gave you," she says. "He better be back by the morning."

I nod, hoping so badly that he will be.

I head to my room, where it's dark and cold because I left my window open. I call Ivy and G-mo. Neither of them pick up.

I stare at my ceiling, and it starts to fully sink in that I don't know where the hell my brother is. I press my palms together and interlock my fingers. I pray—no, beg God to watch over Tyler, wherever he is, to make sure he stays safe, to make sure he gets back to us okay.

My eyes get all heavy and tired, but I try to force myself to stay awake, replaying my conversation with Tyler, replaying the screaming, replaying the gunshots. I tell myself I don't deserve sleep, and I just stare at my alarm clock, hating myself a little more every time the numbers go up, waiting for him to come back home.

· **8** ·

Before I know it, the sun is slapping me in the face and my eyes are heavy with sleep even though I don't remember closing them for longer than a few minutes. They're sore, and it hurts to blink.

It obviously takes a damn herculean effort to move and think, but I do it the best I can, peeling back the layers of blankets on top of me. It's like at some point in the night Mama came and tucked me in.

I go and see if Tyler's in his room. He's still gone. And Mama is still asleep.

I get back to my room, feeling like I'm being smothered, my heart palpitating. Ivy calls me.

I answer quickly. "Hello?"

"Hey, Marv. G-mo's on the line, too."

"Why didn't you guys answer last night when I called you?"

"Phone died," Ivy says. "And it takes forever to charge. Sorry."

G-mo doesn't even bother to answer the question. "We're officially criminals," he says. "I won't survive in jail. None of us will. But especially not me."

"We're not criminals," I reply, my heart throbbing as I walk to my window to look out onto the street. Four little girls play hopscotch, and Mr. Jennings, a middle-aged man who lives across the street, collects trash in his yard.

"We're criminals by association, according to the cops," he says back. "They've already started arresting people who were at the party."

I pause. "We're not going to jail," I say. I back away from the window when Mr. Jennings makes eye contact with me.

"Anything new on Tyler?" Ivy asks.

And I struggle to say the words for the first time. "Tyler..." I stop and exhale.

"Marvin?"

I pause a bit longer, a lump in my throat. "Tyler is missing."

"What do you mean he's missing?"

"He's missing. He never came home. I don't know where he is."

I hear one of them gasp.

"I don't know what to fucking do," I say.

"Do you think he was arrested? The police have been arresting people!" Ivy says.

I hang up on them, annoyed.

What really went down? *Did* Tyler get arrested? Or worse—and my heart almost stops at the thought—did he get caught in the cross fire?

But if I'm alive and my friends are alive, Tyler has to be alive, too.

I change into a pair of joggers and a plain white T-shirt. The air starts to smell of burnt toast and cigarette smoke, and that means only one thing: Mama is finally awake and waiting for Tyler and me in the kitchen, probably thinking that he should be home by now, even if he did stay the night at someone else's house. I wonder what she'll do when she realizes he isn't here.

I build the courage to go into the kitchen and face Mama. "Good morning," I mumble to her. Her back is turned to me, hair rollers entangled around her head. She just exhales a puff of smoke, side-eyeing me like she's a step ahead of me.

She's got plain bagels in the toaster, and she's got a shot glass, a bottle of whiskey, and a stick of butter, and I even notice she has out Dad's favorite cereal: Cap'n Crunch. And I know now that something is really bothering her. Mama hasn't bought Cap'n Crunch since before Dad got taken away.

She's too quiet, and I know she's thinking about Dad. At least she isn't thinking about Tyler. There's no use in having both of us worry about him.

I look down at my hands, where I'm holding my phone. He could call at any moment from a friend's cell or something. Or even better, he could come walking through the door.

●

After eating, Mama and I find our way to sitting on the dingy and holey little red sofa in the living room, watching the news. The picture on the television screen is grainy and wobbly and the signal is poor, like it belongs in the home of a ghetto family.

The newscaster is a white woman with straight white hair. "Live report in Sterling Point," the lady says, her voice nice and calm and firm. "Yet another tragedy in the area. I'm standing in front of an old Pic-A-Rag market, where last night a party ended in a shooting, leaving two dead and three severely injured."

The camera zooms in on the inside of the building, and

I glance at the wall where Tyler was in a chokehold. I see police officers with gloves gathering all the debris, trying to scrape up DNA. And then the camera zooms in on a series of ambulances. EMTs are hauling away two bodies in blue bags.

The camera zooms out and pans back to the woman, a close-up shot, as if all of this is being played like a movie. "Authorities say eighteen-year-old gang member Johntae Ray Smith and two unnamed, underage suspects were arrested at the scene last night."

Mama cuts off the news and flips to watch thirty seconds of some soap opera before she turns the TV off completely, and then I realize I'm still staring straight ahead, in absolute shock, as the news report plays over and over again in my head.

Johntae and two unnamed suspects got arrested. And that's all I can think about.

Tyler is in jail. Tyler is in jail. Tyler got locked up and he's in jail. The thought tastes so bitter. It's giving me a prickly feeling all over.

I blink, wiping away at my eyes, about to self-destruct like a grenade, because I may not have gotten killed last night, but this will kill me—Mama will kill me, when she finds out we went to that party and now Tyler's in jail...or worse.

Two dead.

I sit on the little red sofa, familiarizing myself with the holes.

There's a pounding on the door, like metal bars are being used to break the door in. Mama and I freeze.

She gives me a look. Her eyes are cold and helpless, like answering the door is just as fatal as going to a drug dealer's party the night of a shooting. She gets up, looks through the peephole first, and then cracks the door a few degrees, enough for natural light to shine in on her bare feet. She opens the door wider, and two white detectives stand there with aggressive expressions. One of them is rather slender and has slicked-back blond hair, and the other is bald with a round, extended belly. The two of them, standing here together, means only bad news.

"Does Tyler Johnson live here?" the one on the right asks boldly, showing his badge. Detective Bills.

Relief floods through me. Tyler can't be in jail if the cops are looking for him. But then, where could he be?

Mama nods, saying, "Yes. He's my son. Why?"

I squint to read the other one's name. Detective Parker.

"Are you Tyler Johnson?" the bald one, Detective Bills, asks me, raising his eyebrow, like he's just caught me red-handed, like I am on America's most-wanted list.

I shake my head fast. "He's my twin."

"Twin?"

"Yes," I say, "my older twin. Only by a couple minutes, though."

"And who're you?" Detective Parker asks, his nose wiggling, showing all the stress wrinkles on his face from years of locking up boys who look like me.

"Marvin," I answer.

Detective Bills pauses. "Ah. Marvin. Do you know Mr. Johntae Ray Smith?" He adjusts his black tie.

Mama stares at me with shock and horror washing all over her face, like a river after a storm.

My head hurts and my pulse pounds harder, heavier, faster. I can feel thudding in my ears. "No, I don't. Sorry."

The detectives look at each other in disappointment.

Mama asks, "What's going on, officers?"

Detective Parker coughs. "Have you watched the news today, ma'am?"

She looks at me and then back at them. Mama nods. "Yes." Her voice moves slow, panicked.

"Please just give us a call when your son comes back."

Mama tries to catch her breath, like her thoughts are running marathons and she's drained. "For what?"

"An anonymous tipster said your son was somehow involved with the events at the old Pic-A-Rag market."

Mama shakes her head. "He was out working on a school

project last night. That's not true. It's not true. He's being falsely accused."

"Ma'am, all people involved in what happened at that party are equally guilty. Just give us a call, please, when he's returned."

The detectives leave Mama with a business card, and then they're on their way, back to wherever they came from. Perhaps some mountain, highly elevated above Sterling Point, where they can sit on their porches and overlook the entire city, taking notes and keeping track of all the boys and girls who are stuck in the hood, waiting to get in their way when they try to get out.

It's not like Tyler to just *disappear*. He's full of surprises, and we haven't been as close lately, but this is something he'd never do. I want to fucking cry, but I swallow and blink the tears away. I can sugarcoat and decorate my thoughts in any way I want to feel better, but nothing will help because my brother is fucking missing.

Mama waits, stunned, with the door wide open before she slams it shut and comes after me, rage and terror beaming from every inch of her.

"That boy is dead," she puffs out, reaching for her carton of cigarettes. "Go and get him from wherever he's hiding. I'm getting my belt ready. I'mma beat that boy into another country."

All I want to say to Mama is *Keep calm. He's innocent until proven guilty*. But no words come out.

And the guilt is all over *me*, wrapped around me like a human-sized condom with no mouth hole.

I go to my room to grab my sneakers, but in the hall, I stop in front of Tyler's room. All I see is his bedspread draped on the floor and a window cracked, with a row of half-drunk Gatorades on the ledge. There's a breeze from the window that tickles the side of my face, and I can feel the panic boil my blood more than before.

Two dead and three severely injured. Remembering the newscaster's words sends chills up my spine, and I pray to God that Tyler isn't one of them. If anything, at this point, jail is better than being one of the dead or injured. I can't get my stomach to simmer and settle down. Tyler is missing. Tyler is missing. Tyler is fucking missing.

· 9 ·

I take a deep breath and wipe my eyes and send Ivy and G-mo a text asking them to meet me in the park, and I get instant replies saying they'll see me there.

The park is really just a fenced-in sandbox with a basketball court around the block from Sojo High. There's a convenience store across the street, so it's also the place where the employees take their smoke breaks. The park has an illustrious history. First, it's where Ivy was conceived. Second, it's where a famous graffiti artist once took his life after going through a difficult divorce—one that he really wasn't prepared for since he was an alleged hard-core nine-to-fiver who spent too much time drinking and gambling in alleyways. And finally, it's also where I met Ivy and G-mo. So, all this is to say that the park is *our* place.

As I pedal, I replay Dad's most recent letter in my mind, because it is essential for me to not have a nervous breakdown, and the wind knocks me into gear, pushing me faster along the holey sidewalk, while the sun bakes me to a crisp, my T-shirt sticking to my back like papier-mâché paste.

DATE: SEPTEMBER 23, 2018

TO: MARVIN D. JOHNSON (MY SON)
FROM: JAMAL P. JOHNSON
PRISON NUMBER: 2076-14-5555
MESSAGE:
Son,
   It's Daddy.
   You ever feel like a superhero? Sure you have. I know what it means to be Superman now. What sucks is, like most superheroes, people will always think you're a villain—the bad guy—when you think you're being a hero. I bet you'd

be a supercool superhero. Who would you want to be? Black Batman? Then I could be Black Robin, and we could be a team of black heroic villains all the time, conquering the world.

I see now why they take away your shoelaces and belts and stuff when you get here. I thought it was so they could still hold something over you, so they could take away your dignity. No. It's so you can't kill yourself no matter how bad it is, no matter how bad you feel. I guess making you live is part of the punishment.

It's funny and sad to say this, but when I sit around in the courtroom, it feels like I am free, even though I am not. I feel like the lawyers and the judge and everyone are doing a job that involves me, but I am not involved. It's only when they drag me back to my prison cell that they remind me that I am involved and that I am the devil.

I've been forgetting a lot lately. I don't know if I told you yet, but they've

*got me my own lawyer, too. She's a nice
white lady. She makes me feel like I am
a real person, like I can choose to be a
hero or a villain as I please. And it's nice
because I want to feel like I am a real
person—a good person, because I am.*

So much love,

Daddy

My mind goes blank as I approach the park, everything around me starting to spin.

I hop off my bike quick, slamming it into a rusty bench, my heart ringing in my ears, and a couple minutes later I see G-mo and Ivy biking and skating around the corner, panting, the sun illuminating the sides of their faces enough for me to see their troubled expressions, like they, too, share my guilt and shame and anxiety.

They crash their wheels into the same rusty bench and then attack me with questions, their eyes watery and heavy. It gets harder and harder to breathe.

"Are you really sure he's missing?" G-mo says, his forehead wrinkled.

"What would *you* call it?" I say, stale-faced, pacing in a slow and steady circle.

Ivy slaps G-mo on the shoulder. "Nigga, *missing* is *missing.*"

"We have to find him," I say.

Ivy straightens. "Where do we look first?"

"We have to go back to the Pic-A-Rag," I answer.

The three of us pedal and skate as fast as we can. The whole time, my chest feels like thick vines are twisting and tangling inside.

When we make it make to the abandoned Pic-A-Rag building, there's yellow caution tape everywhere, glass littering the ground, the empty windows boarded up, a few bullet holes mazing the outside like the graffiti in the city.

I hop off my bike, allowing it to fall to the ground, watching people walk up and down in front of the building as if this is a normal scene.

I look around, checking for cops. "All right, let's go in," I say, feeling sourness in my stomach.

"Are you insane?" G-mo hisses. "That's illegal, Marvin."

"Illegal?" My brother is fucking missing, and he's over here talking about some *illegal*.

"This is a damn crime scene. Look!" He points at the area around us.

"You know what? Fine. Just stay here and be the lookout. Ivy and I will go inside."

Ivy cuts him some side-eye while shaking her head. G-mo shrugs.

The two of us go underneath the caution tape and walk

into the building, glass cracking and wooden boards splintering beneath our shoes. The inside is exactly how I thought it would look: like a tornado came through and shook everything. Tables flipped upside down, red Solo cups and beer bottles littering the floor, shoes that were left behind. I wander around, careful not to mess up the crime scene and not to put any of my fingerprints on anything. My heart thumps louder, harder.

Only a little natural light from outside shines in through some of the cracks in the walls around us. Pushing through upside-down tables, through the rubble, through the dust, I make my way to the wall where I saw Johntae threatening Tyler. I place my hand on it, running my fingers across the blue paint, cold against cold.

"Nothing over here," I say, replaying the memory from last night so clearly in my mind. I can feel my hands shaking as I step back, taking deep breaths to keep from bursting into flames.

I'm not sure what I was expecting to see. Ghosts. Dead bodies. A wounded Tyler with his arms outstretched, waiting for me to save him. But the Pic-A-Rag is empty.

Ivy grabs me by the shoulders. "We're going to find him, Marvin. He may not be here, but he's somewhere." She gives me this warm grin, but nothing can calm my nerves.

I swallow hard, blinking back tears, as we meet up with

G-mo, empty-handed and back at square one. I want so desperately to believe what Ivy said, but something doesn't feel right.

G-mo and I hop on our bikes and Ivy gets on her skateboard, and we ride down the block a little bit, going toward G-mo's apartment, stopping by places I know Tyler likes to hang around, even looking in alleyways and on the basketball court and on corners where I've seen him before, but he's nowhere to be found.

The sidewalk is narrow, so we're riding single file. Ivy squeezes in on one side of me. "Let's stop at G-mo's and wait for a bit. He's going to turn up, Marvin." She gives me a small smile.

Time is slipping past and I can't waste any of it, so I agree to Ivy's plan.

●

Stepping into G-mo's place, I get a huge waft of spices. His apartment is completely empty, and it feels almost lifeless, even though the walls are plastered with teapots with the Colombian flag painted on them and portraits of the Virgin. We rush up the stairs to G-mo's room in a single-file line, still unsure of what to make of the last two hours of our lives.

And stepping foot inside his room, I burst out in all of my frustration, crashing onto G-mo's New Kids on the

Block–themed bedspread, which smells like a blend of Cheetos and Axe cologne. "WHAT. THE. HOLY. FUCK?"

Once, back in early middle school, my dad got a little too wasted and beat Tyler and me with a broomstick for talking back. But I've never hurt all over—inside and out—as much as I do right now.

G-mo turns on an episode of *A Different World*. It's the one where a hurricane comes and destroys their entire campus, and Ron and Freddie end up confronting their differences while trapped together. Well, there's a hurricane inside me right now, and I'm really wishing Ron and Freddie could be Tyler and me.

We gotta keep looking for Tyler, I think to myself. *Waiting isn't doing anything for anyone.*

I feel beat-up, bruised, and broken down inside. And not even my music or rewatching the Tupac episode of *A Different World* could help me now. They're like Band-Aids that have been soaked too much to actually do anything anymore.

Suddenly, my phone blasts a different ringtone. Anonymous caller. "Someone's calling," I yell in a high voice, inching off the bed quickly, like a fish trying to flop back into water from the shore. My heart flutters. It could be Tyler.

"What?" Ivy says.

"Who is it?" G-mo asks.

I put the phone on speaker and answer.

"Hello?" My voice is scratchy and rough.

There's a brief cough and then the voice speaks. "Aye-yo! Marv-Marv. It's your boy, Johntae." His voice sounds all willful and content, like he's happy to be where he is.

"Johntae?" My chest feels heavier.

"Homie! How you feeling? How you feeling?!"

"Terrible," I mutter. "I'm in a very dark place right now."

"Well, turn on the light."

"Johntae, I'm not in the mood for jokes, and I'm not even sure why *you* are. You're in fucking jail."

"Chill out, fam. What's gotten into your Wheaties this morning? When you've got a heart of darkness like me, jail isn't the worst place to be. I think jail is a lot nicer than you prolly think. A lot easier than being out there, trying to survive on the streets."

"You sound insane," I tell him.

"You're just as sane or insane as I am, fam."

"No. No. No, that's not fucking relevant," I say, shaking my head. "Tyler is missing." I clench my eyes.

"Missing?" His voice is full yet emotionless. "I don't know nothing about that. I was calling to see if Tyler left you the cornflakes for me? That's all I'm talking about, you dig?"

"What the hell are you talking about? Tyler is missing. I

repeat, Tyler is *missing*. And I believe *you* had something to do with it. Where is he?"

Johntae laughs his laugh. "I thought you were fucking with me? Oh. God. That's not good. You serious right now, thug?"

"I solemnly swear. He's legit gone." I grind my teeth. "We just went back to the old Pic-A-Rag market. It's all boarded up and empty."

"Maybe someone's already given him the easy way out."

"The easy way out?" I ask.

"A bullet to the head," Johntae says, hurt and actual emotion finally evident in his voice for the first time.

The possibility hits me. My heart feels like it's pounding its way right out of me.

NO. NO. NO.

WHAT. THE. FOR REAL. FUCK.

THAT CAN'T BE REAL. THAT CAN'T HAPPEN.

My thoughts grab me by the neck and keep me in a chokehold, and I can't breathe, my chest tightening. I go completely silent, grab the phone tighter, hear the metal case make a crackling sound.

And I guess he hears my sniffling as I wipe the wetness from my eyes, because he goes, "Aye, are you fucking crying right now? Man, that shit ain't gon' do nothing right now! And if you looking for comfort, I ain't got none to give."

I don't say anything back. I can't say anything, like it's physically impossible to command words to come out of my mouth.

"Listen. I called you, Marv, because I know you'll listen and understand and, apparently now, will do whatever is necessary to get your brother back."

"Yeah?"

"I need your help," Johntae says slowly. "I've got a thousand-dollar bail. If you can get me out of here, I can help you get Tyler back."

I say, "Deal," without hesitation. I barely have a buck to my name, but I don't care. I'll do anything to have my brother back.

"Go to one-oh-eight Sycamore Lane and talk to my girl. Her name's Faith. She'll help you with bail money."

When I click off from Johntae, I feel like I'm split into bits. Twins are like synonyms that know each other through and through, like the moon complements the stars through a life sentence, like a set of infinite entities who've seen the world together, experienced its pain and oppression, but I can't help but feel, in this moment, like my world is ending over and over again, like time moves backward, like the world flashes between black and white and grainy and clear.

I can't believe Tyler chose to hang out with Johntae and his crew and got onto this path. Mama used to say that a strong man isn't the same as a good one. That a good man is hard to find because the strong ones usually turn bad. She said, "Good ones are good because they set their own paths and never follow anyone else." I wonder where Tyler fits in on her "good man" scale.

I pause a while longer, thinking about the times I saw Tyler with Johntae, and how I told myself what I wanted to hear, focusing my attention on other things—selfish things. Maybe I'm the reason Tyler is missing. Maybe I deserve this—all my worries scarring me.

The air is stale. Ivy's and G-mo's eyes meet mine.

"I know exactly where Sycamore is," Ivy says.

The three of us storm up and head out.

●

When we make it to 108 Sycamore Lane, I end up walking to the shabby wooden door with cracks and a floor mat that says WELCOME, LEAVE THE DRAMA OUTSIDE, and I knock.

I wait, and the entire time I look back at G-mo and Ivy, who stand there with scared and confused faces. All that's running through my head is that Tyler is missing and I have to bail out a drug dealer so he can help me find my brother.

And a moment later, a girl peeks her head through a crack in the door, a shower cap in hand.

It's the girl from the party. Faith.

She has her hair tied back in a single braided ponytail and curiosity on her face. She looks and smells sweet, and one waft of her makes me lose my words.

Her forehead wrinkles. "Can I help you?" I see her dark brown eyes. Dark brown, like umber.

Tyler, Tyler, Tyler. His name echoes in my head.

I put my arm behind my head and force myself to say, "Do—do you know Johntae?" And I can't fucking believe I say *doo-doo*. And I can't believe I ask her this stupid question. Of course she knows him.

Her smile fades, and then there's a frown and an evil look in her eyes. "Why?" she asks. "Who wants to know?"

"Johntae sent me here to, uh, get money for his bail."

"Well, you tell that no-good piece of shit that I said to fuck off next time you talk to him. Say it exactly like that." And then she slams the door in my face.

Feeling my heart pick up speed, I pause and look back at Ivy and G-mo, who both just shrug. Then I knock again, telling myself to get it together as the door opens once more, and Faith stands there.

"Tyler Johnson," I say slowly, so I don't stutter. "Have you seen him?"

"No. I don't know him."

"He's my twin brother and he's missing, and I need help finding him. Please. He was at Johntae's party. You had to have seen him. Please." My voice rises.

"I don't know him," she repeats, even firmer than before, craning her neck sideways. "And I don't know where he is."

"Johntae knows things a lot of people don't, like the secrets of Sterling Point and hideouts that Tyler never told me about." I stop to take a breath, wanting to keep going, but the words dam up in my throat.

I don't think she believes me. "Please," I say firmly. *Don't start crying,* I command myself.

She exhales, licking her lips, and I watch her face change, like she realizes my desperation. She swings the door open all the way. "And why did you come here?" she breathes out over my face, smelling like she's just eaten fresh pineapple.

"I need the bail money for Johntae so he can tell me where my brother is. I don't have it."

I can feel the blood rushing in my ears while I wait for her to say something back—anything.

I know she wants to help me. I can tell by the look in her eyes.

But all she says is "I'm sorry, I can't," before shutting the door again and locking it.

Defeated, I walk down the sidewalk a few blocks with G-mo and Ivy, both of them telling me we'll figure out another way to get the bail money to find Tyler, making lefts and rights when needed, taking in the hideous sight that is my origin story. The cracked sidewalks are like ripped paper bags. And everything, to me, just looks like a mound of trash.

· 10 ·

With no other way to get the money to bail out Johntae, it's now up to me. Ivy, G-mo, and I go back to
G-mo's place to flesh out a plan and collect our thoughts,
and his mom, Lupe—a short brown woman with long, curly
black hair and eyebrows as bushy as G-mo's—makes us
chips and guacamole. I've never had it before and it tastes
amazing, and something about the lime or the cilantro or
whatever else is in it calms my nerves.

My phone buzzes with Twitter and Instagram notifica-
tions. People from school are uploading their pictures from

the party, captioning them everything from *Wild night* to *The night I almost got ganked.* None of the photos have Tyler in them.

I sit in the middle of a brown, scraggly loveseat, Ivy to my left and G-mo to my right. Seventeen years I've known Tyler, and suddenly disappearing isn't something he'd just do. My leg begins to shake from my thoughts, and I let out slow breaths.

I walk over to the window that's across the room and press my face up against it, scanning the vastness and the limits of the city. G-mo's apartment is only on the fourth floor of this apartment building, but I can almost see my house in the distance.

I feel someone creep up behind me. It's Ivy.

"Hey," she says. She takes off her blue jean jacket, revealing an Eminem/Slim Shady T-shirt, and then she starts to fan herself. "I admire you, Marv."

I raise my eyebrows.

She flashes a smile, and I notice G-mo's finishing off the guacamole straight tongue-to-bowl style. "I've never felt as tight with my siblings or anyone as I do with you and G. And I don't mean that on no weird, straight, lovey-dovey shit either. But like family." She looks away. "I don't know what I would do if either of y'all went missing."

I don't even notice I'm crying until I feel the drops roll

down my face. G-mo's mom is in her bedroom, yelling something at him in Spanish. He answers back.

The glass bowl clinks down to the coffee table in front of the loveseat, and G-mo clears his throat. "Remember that one white girl who got kidnapped by her ex-boyfriend and it was like World War Three?"

"Yeah," Ivy and I say.

"How come it's not like that for Tyler? There were squad cars and search parties on every block for days. Even the day she went missing."

"You already know why, fool," Ivy replies, sliding back into her jacket. "Black kids going missing aren't a priority."

There's a beat. "Yeah. The girl's sister is the one who found her, right?" I ask.

"Yep," G-mo answers, nodding and running a hand through his gelled, combed-over hair.

Everything rushes in my head. And I don't feel as helpless, as frail anymore.

"I think we should go back out there and bring him home," I say.

●

We start a three-person manhunt, taking the main road all the way down, going up hills, and cutting through alleyways. To distract ourselves from all the anxiety building inside, the whole time we rap Tupac songs out loud—"Letter to the President," "Holler If Ya Hear Me," "Changes," and "I Wonder If Heaven Got a Ghetto."

"Let's check around Sojo!" suggests G-mo, taking the lead, pedaling fast in front of Ivy and me. "I just saw on Snapchat that some folks went there after the party."

And so that is exactly what we do. We investigate other places, like a local popular chicken and ribs joint that I know Tyler likes eating at, the Methodist hospital in case he got injured, and almost every neighborhood within a ten-mile radius, hoping to find little clues, like shoelaces or his do-rag, but coming up empty-handed.

"I feel like we should be, like, putting missing-person flyers on light posts and trees and front doors and car windshields," Ivy says.

"Nah, that's too risky. If the wrong person finds out there's an unarmed black boy wandering around these streets, he's as good as dead," G-mo says.

Ivy sighs. "Riiiiight." A look of defeat on her face.

We stop by the old Pic-A-Rag market one last time. Still nothing but yellow caution tape closing off all means of entry. This time, there's a police car nearby, but it doesn't look like anyone is inside it.

There's a small food mart directly across the street, sitting rusty and tired. A white family owns it. They're from somewhere up north, and they've got a white woman running the place and security cameras in every square inch of the interior. And I mean, to an extent, I don't blame them. They've been robbed so many times. They've been in the news for weeks. They're fed up.

I, personally, have never had a problem with the lady. Most times, when Mama would take me with her to shop for a few items with whatever little change she had at the bottom of her purse, the lady would greet us with a smile, offer to bag our items, and even wave good-bye. And to Mama, this gave her hope about other kinds of people. To Mama, these little gestures kept her coming back, making this place her go-to for groceries.

And it sucks that I can't remember her name. I mean, on second thought, I don't think she ever bothered to learn my name either. It was just black and white for the three of us.

We stop inside to see if the woman caught anything on any of her surveillance cameras from last night, or even the past couple days—something to give us a lead. I walk into the store, hearing the welcome jingle from a bell atop the door.

Ivy and G-mo wait behind me for a moment. I walk to the counter where the white woman stands, and I squint really hard to read her name badge. "Miss…Deb, umm… my brother, Tyler, has been missing for a while now and I was wondering if I could see your security footage? Like, to see if the cameras caught his whereabouts?" I hold on to such a strange hope—a hope that, in my head, goes a lot like: *Sure, it's right over here.*

But, no. "I can't do that," she says, "and besides, some men in fancy suits already stopped by and got all the tapes."

"The detectives?" I wonder out loud.

She nods, her hands resting on the counter.

I put my head in my hands. I ask her if she has at least seen Tyler. Maybe, at some point, she saw someone who looks *almost* like me come in and buy their whole supply of Arizona Iced Tea and hot Cheetos. But she shakes her gray head.

"Half-off candy!" G-mo says, excited and distracted, breaking off to stroll through the aisle, flipping through the Skittles. Ivy follows to fetch and retrieve him.

A tall boy, about my age, with a duffel bag slung across his shoulder walks into the little store, his hood over his head, brand-new Jordans squeaky clean. But he doesn't come in alone. A white cop follows him. It's a casual sort of thing. The kind of thing where everything is just so coincidental that you don't think much of what's unfolding before you.

The boy walks down the half-price candy aisle also, and for some reason he sets his duffel bag down. He browses up and down the aisle, in careful selection. I watch him as he takes steps forward and then steps backward. And then he trips over his bag, sending Ivy and the whole rack of half-price candy tumbling to the floor. Everything is loud and clattering, putting the policeman and the cashier on alert. And without hesitation, the cashier presses the blue flashing panic button next to the cash register, even though there's already a cop in here, even though there's nothing to even panic about. It was just an accident.

This isn't going to be good, I think to myself, feeling it all over, like an aching bolt of lightning inside me. And I'm suddenly remembering back to years ago, when I first heard of a black kid getting killed by the police for—and I quote—"playing loud music and disturbing the peace."

I run down the aisle to check on Ivy and help pick her up from the floor, her hands wrapped around her head.

The cop and the cashier run over, too, and the cashier slips on a few bags of Tropical Skittles. Her head hits the floor hard enough to bleed, no, hard enough for a concussion, no, hard enough for all our melanin to be blamed.

The police officer clutches his side as he bends down, saying, "Ma'am, are you okay? Ma'am, are you okay?"

And I just stare as I lift my friend up, thinking—*Man, there are three people on the floor. And all you see is this white woman.*

The woman has a split on the side of her head, and blood

starts to ooze out. She bites her lip in pain, shaking her head, her bottom lip trembling like she saw a ghost and it knocked her down or some shit.

"Oh. My. God," the boy says, confused, his hood falling off his head.

And before the boy can scoot closer to the woman to check on her, she tosses her hands up and says, with so much irritation in her voice, "I'm all right—"

"That doesn't look so good," the cop interrupts, examining her head.

G-mo places a hand on my shoulder and Ivy lowers her head, taking off her Los Angeles Lakers hat. And the three of them are not looking at us, and everything inside me is saying to run.

The cop helps the lady stand up.

"I think he was trying to rob me. He looks like one of them hoodlums who came in here the last time," the lady says, holding her head. And I think, *Well, maybe it's a concussion talking.* 'Cause I certainly didn't see any sign that he was trying to rob this place.

Ivy, G-mo, and I exchange looks.

The cop kicks the boy in his ankle as he tries to lift up from the ground. "What's in the bag?" he shouts.

"Sir," the boy says softly, his hands at his sides, "I didn't steal anything. And I wasn't 'bout to either. I promise."

"What's in the bag?" the cop repeats, louder.

"My bag?"

"Yes, your goddamn bag!"

"CDs," the boy answers, "just CDs. That's how I'm funding my college." And he points to the words running across the front of his hoodie: PENN STATE.

The cop snags the bag from the boy as he stands. He unzips it and turns it upside down, dumping everything out all over the candy-covered floor. Sure enough, a few dozen loose homemade CDs fall out, and so does a little dime bag of weed.

The cashier woman walks to the freezer and pulls out a pint of Ben & Jerry's ice cream and puts it to the side of her head. Then she walks back to the front of the store, trusting that the cop will get everything settled.

The cop picks up the dime bag, shoves it in the boy's face, and then puts it in his uniform pocket. His dispatch radio is giving him orders, but he doesn't listen. "You forgot to mention the part where you've got drugs in your bag, too," the cop says. He blinks his pale blue eyes faster.

"But...sir...can I...?"

"Shut up!" the cop barks, coming closer to him.

I can feel my heart beating in my chest, and the three of us take steps back, crushing packs of M&M's and gummy bears, wanting more than ever to flee this place but not wanting to leave the poor kid all alone.

I slip out my phone quick enough to snap a photo of the boy and the officer to post in case things go horribly wrong. And I think maybe this is my subtle way of showing the boy that I see him, that I am here, that he's not alone in this—a boy, with a tear-streaked face, miming with his hands that he has an explanation to stay alive.

"But, sir," the boy says.

"You deaf? I said shut up!" The officer kicks the boy in the ankle again, harder this time. The cop rolls his eyes and coughs two words: "Damn thug."

"No, you don't understand," the boy says. He has this confused expression, like he's unsure of what's actually happening. He struggles to collect all of his CDs from the floor, like maybe he's worried about them getting scratched up.

"Boy, sit your ass back down."

"I promise I wasn't trying to rob this place. I was just getting some snacks. See—look," the boy adds, reaching into his pocket—maybe too quickly, too black, I don't know, but in seconds, the cop shoves the boy into a rack of chips and then body-slams him to the floor. Face-first.

We jump back as we hear the smack.

There's blood and another crunching sound, like bones

being split in half, ringing in my ears. The cop has the boy tied in a submission lock, his arms twisted tight behind him, the boy crying real tears now and screaming, fighting out of the hold.

"Yo!" G-mo yells at the cop. "You're hurting him. He wasn't doing anything to you. Let him go, man."

The cop ignores G-mo, still slamming and kicking the boy around like a rag doll, a plaything. A thing to be brutalized.

"OH MY GOD. WHAT THE FUCK! WHAT THE FUCK!" I find myself screaming this over and over again as everything happens in front of my eyes, open wide—so wide.

"Stop it!" Ivy screams, picking up candy packages and throwing them at the cop's head. "He's just a kid."

And that rings in my head: *He's just a kid.*

He's just a kid. He's just a kid. He's just a kid. He's just a kid.

The cop yells, "Everybody shut the fuck up." He looks at the three of us. "You three better get out of here before you're next."

And now I'm wondering: *What does* next *mean? Next to be treated like a punching bag or an animal? Next to lose my life?* I could fucking throw up right now.

The cop slaps some handcuffs on the boy, and the boy wails, trying his best to break free.

"Goddamn thugs think you own this place. Fuck it. You're gonna learn a lesson today."

My gaze falls to the floor, and I watch blood pool around the poor boy's mouth, desolation in his eyes, and he's coughing and crying and choking and screaming and choking and crying and coughing and begging for this torture to just stop, until he falls silent, beaten unconscious.

My heart shatters into a billion pieces, my thoughts shifting and sorting, one at a time, unable to place themselves. Because nothing makes sense right now.

· 11 ·

The officer lunges out on us, pushing Ivy back onto the floor. He grabs me by my collar and squeezes, his grip feeling like a nylon rope around my neck.

G-mo tries to pry the cop's hands away from my neck. "You comply when I command you to do something. You hear?" the officer barks as he tightens the grip on my collar, and I feel a bone in my neck crack.

"Holy shit, what the fuck is going on?!" Ivy shouts.

"Get the hell off him, yo," G-mo says, still trying to pry away the cop's hands.

"Somebody, help! Lady, help!" Ivy shouts back to the cashier. She does nothing. Just stares. Just fucking stares.

And I'm left peering into this man's eyes, somewhere between cobalt and iceberg, 'cause his glare is the coldest thing I've ever felt. I see all the hate trapped inside them.

He yanks harder at my shirt and then his hands go to my pants and pockets, in search of something.

"He ain't got nothing in there," Ivy shouts, helping G-mo try to wrestle the cop's hands from me, his arms flexing, the veins in his biceps looking thick. His weight is just too much for them.

The officer shoves me back, pinning me against a rack of something that I can't see, and it pierces my back hard. Then, in a moment, there is a fist punching my gut repeatedly, a knee to my crotch, and I'm tossed to the floor, hitting my face hard, and I feel the impact all over.

He's trying to put me in handcuffs, but I wiggle, trying to break free. I tell myself to win this power struggle because that's what this is: the ultimate power struggle. G-mo and Ivy are screaming for me, still trying to get this cop off me.

"You trying to resist, boy. You wanna resist, huh?" the cop keeps saying on a loop.

He squeezes my hands hard behind my back, and my skin is on fire. My heart is pounding in my chest, beads of sweat falling into my eyes.

"That's enough, Joe," the cashier woman finally says. "I think he's learned his lesson today."

And feeling nothing but pain all over and hands on top of my head and moving down my back, all I'm feeling is like I'm seriously going to die without having really lived, and all I am left thinking is: *What lesson did I have to be taught?*

Not to be a concerned individual?

Not to care about someone else's innocent life, the boy lying unconscious across from me?

Not to care about my own life?

Not to be a member of my own race?

I don't know what, but I know that in this very moment I'm starting to really hate myself, really feel sorry for myself, because I've been black for too long, because I've been such a menace to society because of this skin, because of the words that come to mind when some people see me.

"Get the hell out of here and don't come back, or else," the officer says into my neck, releasing me at once. He scowls. The hatred in his voice is scarier than anything I could've ever imagined.

Ivy and G-mo help me up off the floor, and, keeping eyes on the poor boy, we haul ass out of there, seeing cop cars and ambulances flying down the street toward the food mart.

We ride all the way back to the park in my neighborhood, our brains scattered and exploding into a million thoughts.

●

"You okay?" Ivy asks.

I nod at her, not actually feeling okay in the slightest. I'm replaying what happened at the store in my mind, my throat tightening. That could've been my brother, easily. How do I know he isn't already lying somewhere, beaten unconscious, or worse—dead—because he's black and looked at as a threat before actually being *seen*?

"Yo. What the fuck is going on with the goddamn cops, man?" G-mo goes.

"My mama say this world's going to shit," Ivy adds. "That's just all there is to it."

I have to catch my breath. I'm unable to say anything, horrified, still thinking about what just went down, still flinching from this nasty twinge all over me. I feel like my bones are legit on fire. Like someone ran a cheese grater over every single muscle in my body. But I'm reminding myself that I can't allow pain to reign over me. I can't handle another oppressor.

"That was some fucked-up-ass shit. He only had CDs and a dime bag. No one deserves to be beaten like that. He could've died. That isn't punishable by death. What's worse is that that could've been any of us," Ivy says.

"Word," G-mo sighs.

"And we just stood there and ran like pussy-ass bitches," she moans, her chest heaving.

"Ivy, goddamn, how many times do I gotta tell you that I'm a pussy-ass nigga and I like being one?" G-mo shouts. "That's how I keep my life."

"That's 'cause you literally got nine functioning brain cells. You keep being a pussy-ass nigga, and that's what they gon' keep treating us like."

"Whatever, I guess," G-mo says. "When's the damn rapture? Because that was so fucked up."

"Who do you even call when the cops are the ones being the bad guys? Who do you even beg to protect you?" Ivy asks, putting her hands on my sore shoulders.

I shrug. And I have no answer—not a good one, at least. But I know not all cops are bad. Auntie Nicola was one, and I know she's a good person. In her time as an officer, she did a ton for the community: got people the help they needed and made them feel whole and safe—what good cops are supposed to do. I remember Auntie Nicola telling me stories about catching bad guys and how she'd seen some of her colleagues use their power to do some pretty messed-up things to people, but she always made it known that there'd be cops like her on my side.

My mind flashes back to when Tyler and I used to spend our middle school spring breaks with Auntie Nicola in

Indiana. She'd take us to the skating rink on the east side of Indianapolis on the weekend. There was something about picking each other up off the floor when we fell, laughing, that made those times mean everything to me. Tyler's laugh slips into my head. I never thought I'd miss it, as loud and gut-busting as it is, but I do. It's been a while since I've heard him laugh and actually mean it. All the happy, funny, quiet little moments between the two of us growing up get stuck in my head, like me and Tyler just sitting on the ground, putting together thousand-piece puzzles, and making peanut butter sandwiches, saying nothing, just watching each other eat. It's the thought of not getting any of this back that has my chest constricting. Tyler may have strayed away, but I need to find him.

I don't know how long I blank or how long I just sit there not saying anything, staring at a single point, a crack in the street, my thoughts splitting into a million fragments. But, somehow, I snap back together, and I'm on my bike, pedaling fast.

The whole time, I feel like I'm just drifting with no real sense of direction. In the air, the pigeons fly in salute to the pale, rubber sky, and this is what comes to life, like a giant machine built against me, paining me, all the way until I get home to face Mama. I'm going to tell her the truth about everything. About the party. About Tyler. I have to.

· 12 ·

When I get inside, Mama grabs her first-aid kit and applies all kinds of stuff to the cut on the side of my face: rubbing alcohol, peroxide, and some type of fast-healing cream in a little yellow-orange tube. I gasp—not because of the sting, not because she's heavy-handed, but because I have to tell her the truth, and it's making me wince.

"It's all right," she reassures me in a hushed tone. "You gon' be all right. You safe now." She kisses my forehead and thumbs my cheek.

I'm fucking shaking.

I have to take deep breaths and run through all the words in my head, because I don't even know how to say what I'm about to say. I open my mouth, and I almost trip over the words. "Mama, I have to tell you something," I say. It feels like there's a pillow on my face, a pang in my chest. "I don't know where Tyler is," I say. "I thought that I—"

She interrupts me, furrows her eyebrows. "Wait—what do you mean you don't know where he at?"

My stomach twists and turns. I tell her about the party, about Tyler and Johntae, about the gang, about how I lied, about how I'm sorry and how I'm blaming myself for every-thing. Everything.

"After the party, he just vanished," I say. I'm about to throw up.

She cranes her entire body around and rips through her purse for her cell phone, and I know she's about to call the cops again. She's not called this many times in one week since that night Dad got so drunk and high that he crashed their old green Yukon XL into someone's backyard.

Mama holds her hair away from her face as she calls the police to report Tyler missing. I try to remind myself of what Ivy said, telling myself that he's out there and that he's alive and that he's safe. Mama paces while I stand still in agony.

It feels like the world stops rotating.

Mama glances at me, a hand over her heart like at any moment she'll have a heart attack, as she tries to explain everything. I move over to sit on the couch, familiarizing myself with its holes like usual, pulling out cotton and putting it back.

It takes her far too long to get the report filed. I guess if you're black, there are some additional steps that you've got to take. The person's low voice streams out of the phone, and I hear everything. They ask her if my brother is in a gang, if he's been in any trouble with the law lately, if he has any enemies—after each of which Mama says, "No."

When Mama gets off the phone, she has this ghostlike look in her eyes. "We gotta go down to the station and talk to them," she says without looking at me, her head hoisted up. "They got more questions."

I throw on one of Tyler's hoodies, which is stained with his cologne—it's too big, but I need it to consume me, to remind me that he's still out there.

In the car on the way to the station, Mama and I don't say a word. She just sobs as I stare out the window, looking at the lights, and the stars, and the people, too. I can see her glancing at me through the reflection in the window, but we keep quiet, and her silence makes me wish this hoodie really would swallow me into a black hole.

●

When we get to the police station, two cops escort us to the detective's office, walking us through a long hallway, passing other offices on both sides. The offices look like tight glass boxes, letting me see inside them. Some of them are neat, while others are messy as shit, papers everywhere. Voices come through on walkie-talkies, and some cops type on computers. Many of them are just standing with each other in the hallway, staring Mama and me up and down.

We pass by a wall full of photos of missing people in Sterling Point. There're so many of them, so many of them black and brown, and it gets harder and harder to breathe. When we get to the detective's office, a man in a fancy suit with an American flag tie shakes Mama's hand. He offers Mama and me hot chocolate and those mini bottles of water.

I take a deep breath before I chug down my entire bottle. Fuck slow sips.

Mama starts to explain everything, but the detective stops her to say that he was the one who she spoke to on the phone. Then he looks square at me. He puts this sneaky smirk on his face and opens his mouth as he extends his hand. All I can smell is coffee on his breath, and his sweaty palm grips mine.

"And what's your name?" He's talking to me like I'm some little kid. This is already some bullshit, man.

I tell him my name anyway.

"I'm Detective Conaway." He pauses, pointing to his name tag on his desk, papers scattered everywhere on top of it. "I'll try not to keep you two here all night. Okay?"

We don't say anything. I can tell even Mama is ready to slap his smiling ass.

"Well, Marvin, you know that you're essential to the whole investigation, right?"

Mama starts to say something, but he interrupts her.

"I mean the investigation for the party *and* finding your brother. We need your help to put all the pieces together. How does that sound?" He's still fucking smiling at me. I'm not in the fucking smiling mood.

He takes my nonresponse and says, "Okay, let's get started, shall we?" He shuffles through manila folders on his desk and pulls out a blank notepad and a blue pen.

"Why aren't you sending some of these people to find my son?" Mama asks thickly in such a pleading voice. "They ain't doin' nothin' but standing around."

"I understand your concerns, but, Mrs. Johnson, this is standard procedure," the detective says. "We have to know the facts so we know what we're dealing with. Besides, we can't go looking for any missing person when we don't even know where to start our search."

"Can you just ask your questions already?" I say. They both look at me with widened eyes, like they thought I'd snuck out in the middle of their conversation.

The detective clears his throat, reclines in his chair, adjusts his tie, and begins. "Mr. Marvin Johnson, your brother's name is Tyler, huh? And you both attend Sojourner Truth High School?"

"Tyler Jabril Johnson," I reply. Naturally, my voice cracks. "And yeah."

He writes it down and pulls out a recording device. "Standard procedure," he adds. "So...you and your brother were at the party in the abandoned Pic-A-Rag building?"

I hesitate to answer, afraid of saying the wrong thing. He's talking about the fucking party, and all I want is a full city sweep. Everyone should be looking for Tyler.

"Is this how all this gon' be?" Mama says. "'Cause I ain't bring him here to talk about no party. You got questions? Okay, but make sure they're relevant to finding my boy." I can feel all the emotion in her voice, just like I can feel my heart beating in my chest.

The detective's face gets all red and flushed, but he turns back to me. He asks me a bunch of other questions, like if

I know Johntae, whether or not I knew about the guns and drugs in the building, about the raid. And now he's asking me if I'm in Johntae's gang.

I pause, feeling the entire world as it spins faster. I know Mama will be heartbroken to hear the truth.

I swallow down the lump in my throat. "No. But Tyler is." I try my best not to look at Mama, but I hear her gasp, her shaky breath. For years, she tried her best raising us so that we wouldn't give in to the streets.

Detective Conaway leans forward like I've just given him the golden answer. "Excellent."

Excellent? What the hell is that supposed to mean? Is Tyler being in a gang like a pass to not look for him? Just because he fell for the gang life doesn't mean he's not savable, that he's not worth risking everything for.

I pick up the hot chocolate and try to swallow some.

"If I asked you to write down all of the people your brother hangs out with, could you do that for me?"

I look at Mama and she has her head in her hands, and I can tell she's beating herself up inside as much as I am about losing him at the party when I told myself I'd keep an eye on him. I look back at the detective and nod.

I take a few minutes to write down all the names of who I know are in Johntae's gang. "I hope nicknames will do," I say.

"That's totally all right," he answers me.

When I finish, I ask, "Are you going to start looking for him now?"

He glances around the room. "These kinds of things take time. And by the length of the list of names you've provided, it could take anywhere from forty-eight hours to up to a week after interrogation."

I sit up straight. "So you should start right now, then." I have to remind myself where I am and who I'm talking to.

"Just a few more questions," Detective Conaway says.

Mama sighs and I try to match hers, finishing off the small Styrofoam cup of watered-down hot chocolate.

He asks me how long I was at the party and if I stayed the whole time.

"I stayed the whole time, until everything went down." My chest is tight.

"So, there was a shooting that took place before authorities arrived at the scene. Where did you last see Tyler, then? In the midst of everything?"

Mama makes a grunting sound like she's going to say something, but doesn't.

"No. Tyler didn't have anything to do with the shooting. He's innocent and he's missing, but you're still talking about a shooting." I shake my head. It gets fifty degrees hotter in here.

He scribbles as he asks me to recount the last conversation I had with Tyler. It's been replaying in my mind over and over again, and I will never forget seeing him angry and afraid, telling me to leave him alone.

I smell Tyler's scent again, remembering I'm wearing his hoodie. There's a moment of silence before the detective asks, "How much influence did the gang have on your brother?"

A lot is what I should say, because it's the truth, but I don't want to say it out loud. "I don't know" is what I say, feeling the lie run through my body.

"I'm sure you're aware of the lives lost at the party, correct?"

"A little," I answer. I've been forcing myself not to think much about it, because I don't want to think about Tyler being one of them.

Before Mama and I leave the station, the detective has us write down our contact information and all the places Tyler could be. Five or so minutes later, I leave the police station with Mama. Neither of us says it out loud, but we both know we're going to have to look for Tyler ourselves if we want him to be found.

●

Back at home, Mama stays on the couch, talking on the phone with Auntie Nicola about everything. I can hear her voice as I lie across my bed, trying to sleep, but I can't.

I'm looking at my dingy, dark ceiling, praying to God over and over again, asking for a lead, a sign—something.

A sign doesn't come, but I know I need faith that Tyler will be safe. I try to close my eyes, letting this very moment hang in the air for a while, allowing myself to breathe and slow my thoughts. Then, Faith slips into my head. I hop up out of bed and slip into my nearest pair of shoes, and without saying anything to Mama, I climb out my window.

· 13 ·

It's been over twenty-four hours since Tyler went missing, and the moon hangs from its neck in the darkened sky. My thoughts echo like shadows behind me as I mull over the very fact that I'm part of the blame for Tyler's disappearance. If I'd just kept a closer watch on him, I wouldn't have lost him. I know it.

When I arrive at Faith's place, there's a light on in the living room, and through the window I can see a shadow of her dancing, the music so loud I can hear it from the porch.

I walk up to the door and knock hard, looking around me, up and down the street.

The music clicks off, and I hear a latch being undone on the other side.

She opens the door a little bit, just enough for me to see her eyes.

"Hi. It's me—Marvin Johnson," I say, waving and offering a slight grin, as if I'm simultaneously trying to assure her that I come in peace, but also in so much damn panic.

She opens the door all the way so I can see her. She's in sweatpants and a tank and with no makeup, not like how I remember her at the party, but she's still fine as hell.

"What're you doing here?" she says in a confused voice, scanning around outside, too. She grabs her elbows as a chilly gust of wind blows.

My heart thumps loudly. "Please. I need your help."

She pauses, and I can tell something inside her is fighting the urge to slam the door in my face.

"Come in," she finally says, eyes searching up and down the block. "No one's home. My mom's working and my step-dad is probably either passed out in an alley somewhere or at a casino."

Her house smells like old grease and candle wax. Everything is brown and gold and beige and beautiful. She's got a bunch of black celebrity paintings all over her house, like

125

Tupac, Biggie, Beyoncé, and Rihanna, and even older ones, too, like Diana Ross, Gladys Knight, Janet *and* Michael Jackson, and Prince. Everything is clean and crisp, like it's brand-new—even the sandy-brown carpet. I follow her to the couch like an amazed little kid at a museum. And I try to hold off from blinking because I don't want to miss a single second of this moment.

And then she clears her throat and cuts on some music again. The first song that plays is "Keep Ya Head Up" by Tupac. She likes Pac, too. She lowers the volume before she sits next to me on a brown leather loveseat. It's quiet for a moment, except for Tupac in the background: *Look to my future 'cause my past is all behind me. Is it a crime to fight for what is mine?*

"She taught herself," Faith says, pouring two glasses of iced tea. "My mom painted all those celebrity paintings. That's how she stayed out of the streets. Painting saved her, and it left her with a gift." She pauses and smiles. "One day, I think I'll be as talented as her. Even though she's out driving one of the city buses now."

Faith hands me a glass. And I take a huge gulp, cringing inside from the sweetness, but it quenches my thirst. "Those are dope!"

She smiles, but something about her seems stiff.

"So about Johntae and bail and finding my brother," I say, brushing my hands on my pants.

Her smile fades. "I can't help you." She sighs, looking away. "As much as I want to, I can't."

"Why? He specifically told me to go to you for his bail money."

"He still thinks I'm holding on to his savings. I used it to pay for my mother's surgery. She had to have a device implanted because of her heart failure. I never told him because...well..." She stops and looks at her palms. "If I did, he would send somebody to hurt me."

I stay quiet.

"There's a special kind of pain that comes with being with him. And he has these mood swings and I never know how to keep up. And I'm trying to figure out how to detach myself from him. For years, I thought of myself as a collection of *almost*s and *could be*s, but I've realized so much about myself."

"What do you mean?"

"Like I'm going to get out of here, out of this place, out of Sterling Point—finally get away from Johntae. I'm going to online school right now, but I'm trying to transfer to an art school in New York. I've realized that I've got so much potential to be somebody someday." She takes a breath.

The music switches from Tupac to Alicia Keys.

"He holds you back, huh?"

"Johntae has these really high highs and these really low

lows, and then one day, everything boils up and he comes crashing down. And more often than not, I'm the one he's crashing down on. And once he finds out about his money… well, I just have to start sleeping with my pocketknife under my pillow again."

"I'm sorry." I want to offer my protection, tell her that I won't let anything happen to her—but I know Faith is capable of saving herself. She's been doing it since before I met her. And besides, I couldn't even protect my own twin brother.

"No," she says. "I'm sorry that I can't do much to help you."

"It's okay," I say, lying to her and to myself. Nothing is okay right now, but I have to pretend that it is for my mental health. I have to pretend that I'm going to come up with the bail money and I'm going to pretend that I'm 100 percent confident I'll find Tyler.

"Why do you think getting Johntae out will help?" Faith asks, running a hand through her hair.

"Tyler was hanging around Johntae's crew. Johntae has to care about Tyler in some way, right?" I say, trying to ignore the nagging feeling in my gut that I'm lying to myself. "He'll help. Besides, he'd know Tyler's whereabouts. Johntae has people everywhere."

"I know Johntae like the back of my hand. I don't think he'll help you, Marvin."

"I thought I knew Tyler like the back of mine, too, but…"

I stop and look into her eyes, which are deep and brown. "Finding him means everything—*everything*—to me, and bailing out Johntae to help is the only next step I have."

Faith stares up at the ceiling fan. "Sometimes missing people leave clues behind. Have you found anything?"

I sigh and then shake my head.

"The clues don't have to be physical," she says. "Everything you need to know about where Tyler's gone could be in Tyler himself."

"Yeah," I say, puffing out air.

"Yeah, what?" she asks.

"Tyler—he's been really different recently. He's been distant. He's been breaking all the rules."

"Rules." She laughs slightly, like the word tickles her tongue. "Maybe he's not missing. Maybe he ran away. Maybe he was sick of the rules. Maybe all the pieces inside him fell apart." She's the second person to tell me this, after Ivy, and it still doesn't make me feel any better.

I think for a second. "That's not something he'd do."

"People have their ways of surprising us." Her eyes are the only stars I see now, and I cling to them like they're the only sources of light that'll be given to me in this dark tunnel. "Everything will be all right."

I don't think everything's going to be all right. But it's still nice to hear it.

The next day, Sunday, it's almost physically painful to stay in my house; it's so tense and quiet. I sit in my room in silence for a while, a tender soreness in my stomach and arms. I pull up Tyler's Twitter page and scroll through his photos in a selfish attempt to scrape up some happiness. And it almost works until I come across this one photo I haven't seen in years. The photo is of us wearing Transformers costumes to our fourth-grade Halloween party—he was Bumblebee and I was Optimus Prime—and suddenly there's a weight on my shoulders and an emptiness inside me that I just want to fucking go away.

Down the hall, in the kitchen, Mama tells me that the police said they've been searching and interrogating people, and they may or may not have a lead.

Mama's face is like a thesis, and I know every sentence. The lines on her face are telling me she feels exactly how I do.

●

Monday comes around, and I'm running through all the clothes in my closet to find the perfect thing that matches how I feel on the inside. I end up going with some black joggers and a John Cena hoodie Tyler got me from a donation center as a joke one year because he knows how much I hate WWE.

Mama says a prayer before I head to school, asking for the Lord to give wisdom and knowledge to the police looking for Tyler, and before the two of us can say *Amen* in unison, we're both a hot-ass mess of tears and sobs. We hug it out for the longest, and man, I wouldn't mind if this would last longer.

"It's gon' be a'ight. They gon' find him and everything's gon' be a'ight," Mama says to me, and it's only a little bit reassuring to both of us.

I grab my backpack and slip into some sandals, and then I'm out the door. When I get to school, I've got about thirty seconds before the first bell rings for class. G-mo and Ivy are waiting for me at my locker, phones in their hands.

I nod at them, not really able to return their stares. I know I've been ignoring their calls and text messages. "Hey." I shove my backpack into my locker and pull out my textbooks.

"What's going on?" Ivy asks.

"What do you mean?"

"Where've you been?"

I just shrug, and they exchange looks.

"We're worried, Marv," G-mo says, placing a hand on my shoulder and offering a small smile. We haven't been this serious around each other in years. Not since G-mo's dad got deported.

"Thanks," I say, trying to ignore the thick ache in my chest.

The bell rings, and we're late to English, but Ms. Tanner doesn't even care. She knows what's going on—everyone does at this point. And she lets the three of us slide in without making a big deal about it like she normally would.

The entire class is whispering during Ms. Tanner's lesson on vocabulary words. And I know they aren't talking about how cool the words are. I know they're talking about me and about Tyler.

Ms. Tanner rolls out an old-school TV and VHS player to make us watch *Antigone* by Sophocles, telling us that we have to actually pay attention because this will be part of our final exam. If the play were actually hopeful, it wouldn't be so bad to watch. I just fucking need some sort of hope right now.

But no.

Spoiler alert: EVERYBODY DIES.

And that's what really gets me. That's all I'm thinking about: death.

And I feel sick to my stomach, like at any moment I'm going to hurl.

Before the end credits start to roll, I get up from my chair and sneak out the classroom toward the restroom. The bathroom's oddly empty, one white dude pissing a river behind me. I stare at myself in the mirror, splashing handfuls of cold water on my face. I look—and feel—like a slobby, sloppy mess.

"Be strong, bro," the guy says to me once he stops peeing and washes his hands.

I nod, unable to speak without the pain pouring out.

"Sometimes it's hard to hear people tell us to stay strong. But you never know how strong you really are or can be until it's the only choice you have," he adds, straightening his Sojo High jacket.

The guy grabs a handful of paper towels and walks out of the bathroom, leaving me all alone in this place that smells like shit, leaning over a sink full of murky water.

●

I'm exchanging books at my locker when I hear a voice behind me.

"Mr. Johnson," Principal Dodson says. "May I have a word?" And he raises his eyebrow hard, like he's demanding and not asking.

I follow Dodson to his office. I stare at his chest 'cause today's tie is mustard or egg-yolk yellow, and today his office smells like eggs, too.

And on his walls are pictures of white students who have graduated and gone on to some of the best colleges in the nation.

"Take a seat, Mr. Johnson."

I sit in my usual place.

He sits on the edge of his desk, looking down on me like he's about to give me a whack or something, but he just breathes his egg-salad-sandwich breath all over me.

"What's going on?" I bunch up all the muscles in my face, bracing myself to hear some spiel about how Tyler deserves to be missing or something shitty like that.

"Are you aware that Ms. Tanner signed you up for an interview with MIT at the college fair on Thursday?"

I forget to breathe for a moment. "No, sir?"

"No, sir, what, boy?" he shouts, and I flinch a bit.

"No, I was not aware."

"I've tried calling the MIT admissions office, and they won't allow me to cancel your appointment with their admissions representative. You know what that means, boy?"

A confused pause. My mind trips on the thought of even having an interview with MIT. And in my head, I stumble on the idea of not being emotionally ready. And so I just sit and stare and breathe and wonder and forget that I have to answer.

"I know you hear me talking to you," he says with a sneer, clutching a coffee mug, his face wearing irritation. "I said, do you know what that means?"

"No, sir." I flinch and suck in my lower lip.

"That means you have to do it anyway. That means you

have to get your act together." His voice gets louder and heavier, ricocheting around in my ears. "That means you have to put on the face that everything is all right. No missing brother sympathy cards in your hand. You go in there and do whatever it is they tell you to and answer whatever it is they ask and act right so they won't think I run a complete shit show of a school."

My head nods. "Yes, sir." There's a warmth in my stomach, and my hands are a little clammy.

"That means on Thursday, you're no longer Marvin Johnson. You're just another black boy trying to get into MIT."

And I have no words to say, not even the standard military-style *Yes, sir* and *No, sir* I always offer him. I'm all confusion, with the heaviest heart in the universe. I look away, feeling compelled to detach my gaze and stare at the white walls. Guilt is wearing me down because I'm here and Tyler's out there, still missing. And then, almost without me noticing, my head nods for the final time.

I gather my stuff and shuffle out of his office, feeling like the ultimate cyborg of emotions. Like I've been split open in a dozen places and stuffed with darkness.

I run to my next class before the bell rings. The hallways are empty and narrowing and smell kind of sweaty, and yet they still remind me of the infinite sadness running in my blood—these walls closing in on me. I'm glad that I have the chance to interview with MIT, but I'm sad because my interviewing with MIT will do nothing to help Tyler.

●

After trigonometry with Mrs. Bradford, Ms. Tanner stops me in the hallway, and she has this look on her face like she knows she's about to be nosy but also wants to just check in, kind of like she deserves to know everything about me 'cause she got me an interview...with MIT.

"Mr. Johnson," she says, offering a warm and endearing smile. "A word, please?"

Just one is what I really wish I could say. "Sure." As soon as it slips out, I know I'm being shitty. She's just trying to help me, but I can't help but be pissed. I can't really see past all the pain and sadness of my brother being missing.

"I hope you're feeling all right." She exhales, walking closer to me, standing in the doorway of my trig class. "You were out of it in class today, and I just want you to know that I understand everything you're going through. I'm here for you."

"Thank you, Ms. Tanner," I say, looking down at the toes of my shoes.

"And if there's anything I can do to help, just say the word." She puts a hand on my shoulder. "May I ask...How are you feeling, really?" Her face spills concern.

"Like I'm trapped in my mind, like my heart has been ripped out and handed to someone else, like…" I stop.

She rubs my shoulder, squeezing. And she frowns like she's about to break into hysterical tears, but she just stays that way, rubbing my shoulder, then goes in for a hug, whispering, "I am sorry. So, so sorry."

And all I'm wondering is whether she's giving sympathy just because it's her job or because she genuinely cares. Whatever the case may be, I hug her back.

"Also," she sighs, breaking away and reaching into her yellow bag, "this is something I think you'd be interested in. I'm giving these away only to select students." It's a flyer to see a play, *The Piano Lesson* by August Wilson. "You'll earn yourself extra credit, and it'll be good for you. It's not until later in the year, so you have time to think about it."

I blink and turn around, looking over the flyer.

She calls after me. "And, Mr. Johnson. Good luck on Thursday."

I turn back and she winks.

●

After school, I hurry past where Ivy and G-mo are waiting for me, trying to ignore the hurt on their faces and feeling like shit about it—but I know I can't face them right now. Seeing them, talking with them, just forces me to face all the hurt I'm trying to keep down. I hop on my bike, which I notice has a flat tire, the metal rim scraping the ground. And I pedal faster, deeper into the hood.

My phone suddenly buzzes in my pocket. I screech my bike to a stop. A random number pops up. I hesitate to answer.

"Hello?" I say in a somewhat raspy voice.

"Hi, uh, it's me," a soft voice says.

"Faith?"

"Yeah," she replies. "I just wanted to apologize for coming off really selfish the other night."

"No, it's cool," I say. "I shouldn't have put so much on you."

There's a quick beat of silence.

"Are you sure Johntae can help you find your brother?"

"He's the last option I have," I say.

"I hope you're right." She pauses. "Well, are you able to meet me in twenty minutes?"

My eyes widen. "Where? Your place?"

"Yeah."

I turn the bike around and pedal hard.

· 14 ·

'm haunted by the bright sun. I really wish it would get the hell out of my face.

When I arrive at Faith's place, I knock and wait, wrapping my arms around myself.

"Who is it?" I hear Faith say through the door.

"Marvin," I yell. After she opens the door and lets me in, Faith goes to sit on the couch and pats the spot next to her.

"Thanks," I say, sitting down. I notice the coffee table covered in *Teen Vogue* and *Ebony* magazines before looking at her.

Some amount of sadness creeps into Faith's eyes, but she gives me a tiny grin as she runs a hand through her Afro. She changed her hair today, and it looks so pro-black and so beautiful and I'm feeling it.

"You okay?" I ask, knowing damn well everything's not okay.

She nods. "Just a lot on my mind. I'm fine, though."

"Sure?"

She doesn't answer, just gives a small smile and reaches into her long-strapped purse that's on the table. When her hand comes out, she's holding a wad of cash, and my mouth about drops to the floor.

"Faith...I...How?"

"I asked Ms. Bethany for it."

"Ms. Bethany?"

"Yeah. Johntae's aunt," she says. "Johntae's real folks got killed in an accident when he was just a kid. His aunt, Ms. Bethany, has been taking care of him ever since."

"Oh. I didn't know he had any family."

"Yeah. Even folks in gangs have families," Faith says.

I pause. "Thank you, Faith. This means the world to me."

"So what do we do now?" Faith asks, playing with her natural curls. My pulse trembles in my fingertips.

"We go and bail him out so that he can help me look for

my brother," I answer, but I feel so uncomfortable all of a sudden, and I don't really know why.

She gets up, slings her purse over her shoulder, and says, "Let's go."

●

I stare at my message log on my phone, feeling shittier each time I see an ignored text from Ivy and G-mo. I feel terrible for pushing them away, but I'm just so afraid of all the hurt inside me, and I pushed them away as if they were to blame, as if our friendship was just like grains of sand falling through my fingers. I shouldn't have done that. I mean, Ivy and G-mo have been my ride-or-die homies since the beginning, spending many nights talking three-way on the phone about the randomest things that come to mind, and we're always looking out for one another. They're the ones who keep me afloat, too.

"Texts from your friends?" Faith asks, glancing over.

I put my phone back into my pocket. "Yeah."

She watches me like she can see all the shit I'm going through. "I know that when you're hurting, it can be easy to push away the people who care about you—but you're going to need your friends more than ever now, you know?"

I don't say anything, and it's quiet in the car for a long while.

I breathe out through my nose and pull out my phone again and text Ivy and G-mo. I tell them what I'm about to do, that I'm about to bail out Johntae.

And like the true best friends that they are, they don't wait to text me back. They don't even seem mad or upset. Ivy asks if I'm okay, and G-mo sends me a funny Harry Potter meme. It puts a smile on my face.

I gaze out the window, watching all the houses blur past. Some of them are boarded up and abandoned. Others are fancier ones that belong to the rich white folks. My eyes meet the sky, which looks like a beautiful mural of violets and oranges. There's something about it that takes me back to when my dad would drive Tyler and me around in the old SUV on Saturday nights. I miss that, almost as much as I miss the two of them.

It takes an hour, but Faith and I finally arrive at Metropolitan Detention Center, the prison where Johntae is being detained. I'm shaking as I get out the car, and I don't know if it's entirely because of the cool breeze.

This place is dusty and grimy and looks like one of those dungeons from the *Antigone* video we watched in Ms. Tanner's class. Gnats and mosquitoes clog the air, funneling into some of the light posts surrounding the building.

The inside smells like bleach and salt and sterilized depression, and I stand and walk at attention, my eyes racing from right to left, as I take in everything around me. Darkness, orange jumpsuits, and police officers giving us dirty looks.

Faith talks to the officer sitting at the front desk.

"We're here to bail out a close family member," Faith lies.

The woman sits behind a glass wall with a speaker in front of her. She has a huge, pissed-off frown from years of seeing people like us bail out criminals.

"Name?" she booms in an annoyed tone.

"Mine, or...?" Faith goes.

"Both," the lady says, chewing hard on a stick of gum.

Faith gives her the information.

"You may be seated in the waiting area. Wait to be called up," the lady says. I wipe beads of sweat from my top lip, looking around at all the people who're also sitting in the waiting area, which is just a big rectangular room with chairs around the perimeter.

Faith and I sit in the only two empty seats. The room is packed with people and shuffling feet and rustling bags and a wailing baby. My legs shake and my eyes frenzy around the room. Is this what the waiting room would look like at my dad's prison? Will I have to sit in a waiting room like this to see Tyler again, if he's put in jail, too? Is this what I'm going to have to do for the rest of my life—sit in waiting rooms?

"You okay?" Faith asks.

Suddenly, it feels like this room is Hell, and I'm meant to burn in it. "I...just...this—"

"I get it," Faith interrupts me, putting her hand on my shoulder. I gaze into her dark brown eyes, realizing how much she *does* get it. I'm crumbling. I knew that this would be hard, stepping foot inside a prison, because of my dad, but I didn't think I'd begin to fall apart.

"If you want to wait in the car, here you go." She hands me the keys. And I realize that maybe she needs to be the one to bail him out.

I grab the keys. "Thanks," I mumble, and wipe my forehead.

"Yeah, of course," she says with a forced smile. "I'll meet you at the car with Johntae. Okay?"

I wait in the car, taking deep breaths and scrolling through Tyler's Instagram and Snapchat. His Snapchat story is of him chugging a beer and making a face like he just downed a bottle of Windex or something. I know this isn't the first time Tyler has had beer, but seeing him do it on camera makes me feel like this is a whole new side of him I didn't know existed. I wonder what else he does with Johntae and his gang.

After scrolling through Tyler's Instagram for what feels like an hour, I see Faith walking out the door, Johntae close behind her.

Johntae's shouting something—I can see his mouth moving. He holds his junk like he has to remind himself that he's a man.

I get out the car.

"All I'm sayin' is, you couldn't call? You couldn't make sure I was all right?" Johntae shouts.

She rolls her eyes and walks toward me, leaving him behind. "You don't own me," she says over her shoulder.

"Johntae," I call out to him. He doesn't even notice me. He's still staring at Faith, invested in whatever argument they're having.

"What the fuck you mean?" he says, following her.

She presses her body against the side of her car. "You may not want to see it," she says, "but I *am* my own person, and you make me feel broken. Took me a while to realize I'm not." And she just stares at Johntae, taking her life back from him…like in the marrow of her bones there are a thousand cities and hoods being constructed. Like she's learned to love herself and to stop trying to complete herself with Johntae's shattered pieces.

"Whatever!" He slashes the air with his hand, starting to walk away, not saying anything to me.

"Johntae!" I say, running after him. I yank at his shoulder.

"What, lil nigga?" He turns around sharply, his nose turned up.

"Where're you going?"

"I gotta leave this town," he says. "Somebody snitched."

"Snitched? Snitched on who? About what?"

He pauses, looking over my shoulder at Faith, mugging her hard as shit, then glares back at me. He rolls his eyes and smacks his lips. "I gotta go, thug."

"So you played me? All this was a plan of your own? To get me to bail you out, so you can be on your way? You never really meant to help me find Tyler, did you?" I'm screaming, my throat scratchy. The skies still, and everything stops for a second. And he doesn't answer, just looks around, nostrils flared and head tilted back.

I take a short step closer, leaning in. "DID YOU?!" I repeat, pointing at his chest, my fingers in the shape of a gun.

"I'm sorry, Marvin." He sighs, unfazed. "But it was all I could do." And the way he says such a shady apology is just fuel to the fire.

"No. *No!*" I pace around. "I'm not going to let you do this to me." And the breeze becomes stale, and my blood feels icy-hot.

"Go home," he mumbles. "Get out of these streets. They ain't safe. This ain't no amusement park. This is the hood."

"You said you'd help me find Tyler." I feel this sting in the back of my throat.

"I'm just going to tell you the truth," he growls, looking

away. "I don't know where Tyler is." He turns his back and starts to walk off, like that's all I deserve from him, after everything.

I feel like I am sinking into the bottom of the ocean, or in quicksand, my vision blurring, hands itchy and clammy. And the worst part is that I'm not surprised. I knew he didn't know where Tyler was. But it was the only hope I could cling to—and now I have nothing.

I grab his shoulder a second time, and I draw my arm back, and I sucker punch him right in the jaw, and there's a cracking sound as his head cocks back. I bite on my lower lip, my heart beating so ferociously in my chest.

He holds his face, spits on the ground, and glares at me, his eyes wide open and mouth drooling, his chest heaving.

He gives me a mean mug before curling up his fist.

He swings at me, and his fist connects with my face so hard it feels like he fractures my nose. The impact makes me fall to the pavement, my head colliding with the ground littered with tiny stones, beer caps, and cigarette butts.

He turns around and runs, runs, runs away, shouting, "You gon' regret that. You ain't one of us. You ain't nothing but a lil bitch."

Faith helps me up off the ground as blood streams out of my nose like a running faucet.

"Are you okay?" her small voice says.

"I'll be okay," I say, feeling a different, warmer wetness come from my eyes. "Fuck him!" I'm broken like a promise, and all I really want to do is scream and cry on repeat.

And the world blurs and darkens. There's no sound other than my heavy sobbing into a set of arms.

●

Faith drives me to my place, taking the long way there. And I just stare at the moon, like it's cradling me and knowing me through and through, like I'm finding some sort of hope in its luminescence. "Bounce Back" by Big Sean plays on the radio. Faith has the volume on low, but it's still loud enough for the bass to bounce off my pulse. And strange enough, the tears dry on my face. *If you a real one, then you know how to bounce back*, Big Sean sings.

She does her best to keep me calm. "You're not like rest of them—you're not like Johntae. You're so much more," she says. "You're a fighter, so keep on fighting. I'm just…so sorry." It's her saying these things that keeps me from falling apart. And now I'm imagining myself keeping up the fight, finding my brother—imagining a future where all of this just looks like the world's worst joke to my twin and me.

This sky is full of the same old writing, and tonight's story is a warm reminder, something I remember Dad writing to

me in one of his letters: *You'll find light in your darkest times,
always.*

●

Faith stops the car in front of my house, and we just sit
there, staring straight ahead for a moment, listening to
music play on the radio and counting each other's breaths,
our bodies totally motionless. The song's an oldie that my
dad used to play.

"Thank you, again," I say. She's done so much for me, and
I can't help but feel less alone, less filled with anxiety, less of
everything awful. Because of her presence.

"It's the least I could do."

"You're not just saying that, right?"

She puts the car in park. "No." She smiles.

"Good." I nod. "Thanks."

"When you're in a state of despair, not having someone
there to have your back is ugly and awful," she says, lifting
my head up with her index finger. "Seriously. It's the least I
could do."

I stop picking at a hole in the seat. "Oh yeah?"

"Yeah," she murmurs, rolling down her window a little.
"And when you feel lost and alone, lying on your bed, staring
at your phone or scrolling through Tumblr and Twitter and

trending hashtags as if it's meant to bring you peace from all the demons tugging at your head, I know that feeling. We're in this together now. I guess, in some messed-up way, we always have been, even when I didn't know you."

This girl has a heart like a forest, so vast and beautiful, and the twinkle in her eyes captures it. But there's so much more to her than just flesh and bone and beauty.

I stay quiet, letting her words spill over me like water—washing me clean, her words actually doing something, like supplying hope.

"The human heart is like a sponge. There's a way to squeeze out all the hurt you don't want. And somewhere in that hurting heart of yours," she says, "you'll find some strength to go on."

"It doesn't seem like that."

And her mouth straightens. "It never does." She puts her head down on the steering wheel for a moment.

I take a deep breath. "Do you really think he's out there and safe?"

Her head hits the back of the seat, and she stares at a stray cat walking across the street. "If your brother is anything like you, he's a fighter, too. I believe he's out there somewhere. Maybe what happened at the party was the last straw for him, and he wanted to get his shit together, leaving this city behind for good."

"I needed to hear that." I sigh. "Thank you."

She unbuckles her seat belt and leans over slowly, closing her eyes, and kisses me softly on the cheek, which still stings from the punch.

She flickers her long eyelashes until her eyes are wide open—so wide. I watch her settle and relax back in her seat, with a smug and amiable expression. "I like you a lot, Marvin," she says.

"You do?" I sit up. I've never felt so tingly before. It's so dope to hear those words out loud.

"Yeah. You're smart, a little nerdy, and so, so caring. And I adore how you're keeping yourself together. It's so damn hard, losing someone. Besides, my mama told me that boys come with cracks in them and that I'll be able to see them for what they really are once I crack them open. But you're different, and I feel it when I'm around you. These other niggas out here aren't as genuine."

I smile, even though my jaw hurts. "Can I tell you something else?"

"Just spill it already," she mutters through the gap between her front teeth, staring at me.

"I'm not sure if anyone's ever told you this before, but you deserve the world and so much more. You deserve more than the world has—more than what this universe even holds."

"You really think so?" Her eyes start to water up, dimples waving hello.

"Yeah. You are hella bomb, hella beautiful, and anyone in this divided world would be lucky to have you."

Her eyelashes flutter and it's like she's glowing. "That's really sweet, Marvin. Your mama raised you right." She lets out a laugh. Something in her voice makes me think she's never been told this.

"Yeah," I say. Mama taught me to love my blackness and to appreciate the blackness of others.

She puts a hand on my knee. Everything is so hot I have to look away because my face burns, and I'm left thinking: Sometimes people need reminding that they matter, more than they need reminding that they're alive, because sometimes being alive just isn't enough.

I'm really wishing I'd told Tyler that he matters. When I find him, that's exactly what I'm going to do.

· 15 ·

The next morning, Mama has the day off, so she gives me a ride to school, and it feels different.

It's quiet as shit, no sound at all, except for the roaring motor. There're only a few clouds out, but I can smell that smell that says it's going to rain no matter what.

I watch Mama glance in all of her mirrors, like she thinks she'll see Tyler hitchhiking, his backpack on his back, thumb out. Her eyes are bloodshot red, like she's not slept in weeks. She takes a sharp left turn, going the opposite way of Sojo

High, and I'm compelled to speak up. Maybe she's completely lost it. And maybe I'm close behind.

"Where're you going, Mama?" I say, wrinkling my forehead as I give her a worried-as-shit glance.

She looks at me as she speeds up, running through a red light. "I think I just saw him." She has this hopeful look all over her, and it warms me up, and then she pulls up alongside a boy walking into a coffee shop, screaming, "Tyler, Tyler, Tyler!"

The boy doesn't hear at first, and then he takes his hood off, unplugs his headphones, and looks around. This boy's too light-skinned and looks a couple inches too tall to be Tyler.

He gives her a weird look before going into the coffee shop.

She pulls to the side of the road, parks the car next to a meter, and just sobs into her hands, like she's allowing her world to end. And her weeping turns into wailing and her sobbing turns into a frenzied breakdown and her frenzied breakdown turns into her beating away at the steering wheel.

I'm not gonna cry. I'm not gonna cry. I can't.

I reach over, unbuckling my seat belt, and I grab her into a forced hug and I squeeze hard, like it's the last hug we'll feel in this life. And she hugs and squeezes back and kisses my forehead and cheeks, like she thinks I'm going to slip away from her grasp, too.

"You're all I've got right now," she says. "You're all I've got."

●

School seems to last long as shit, and everybody wants to ask me about Tyler, about what I know, about what the cops are doing, and about how it feels to be the twin brother of a missing boy. I try my best to avoid most of it, because it's just too much. I end up missing two of my classes, sitting in the unused, freezing-cold orchestra room, hiding away from everyone, just to clear my mind and let myself cry when I need to. I don't eat lunch with Ivy and G-mo because I can't seem to shut off the feelings knotting in my chest.

When I finally get home, Mama starts making Tyler's favorite for dinner—cheesy broccoli and white rice—and soon I realize it's going to take a lot longer for everything to cook, because she has to take little meltdown breaks, where she cries into the wooden table and smokes a couple of cigarettes. And I wonder why she even decided to make his favorite meal, besides the fact that it's all we have left in the fridge. Maybe it's her motherly way—her far-fetched motherly way—of praying that he'll smell her cooking from afar and come barging through the door.

I head to my room. The rain picks up, and I leave my

window open, just listening to the raindrops pummel the ground. There's something about the sound that completely relaxes me. And I stare at the blank screen of my jank laptop, hoping words will start pouring out of my head so I can have my MIT application finished before my interview.

●

After dinner, we stay at the table, flipping through pictures of Tyler and me. She pulls out Tyler's yearbook photo from tenth grade and kisses it softly, eyes closed.

There's a sudden pounding on the door, beating a familiar beat.

Mama jumps up, her chest heaving. And she looks through the peephole first, like all those times when police visited us.

"Marvin?" she calls, concern oozing into her voice. "Come here." She wipes the corners of her eyes and adjusts her bathrobe. "Stay close."

She opens the door, the wind and rain rushing in. Detective Bills and Detective Parker share an umbrella on the front step, flashing us their badges like we forgot who they are. Detective Parker shouts over the rain. "Ma'am, we're here to inform you that we believe we have found your son Tyler."

Mama holds her heart, attempting a smile, exhaling so hard. She lets go of the door and, touching her cheek, looks back at me. "Thank you, Lord. God is good." She turns to the detectives, a half smile on her lips. Eyes alert—so alert. "Where is he?"

The detectives glance at each other. "Unfortunately, Mrs. Johnson," Detective Parker says slowly, "we've come to tell you that we found his body a few blocks away from the old Pic-A-Rag flea market. We need you to come down and identify the body."

I lose all the air in my lungs. Mama blinks hard, her face wearing shock, before she stiffens and falls to the floor, screaming like she's being tortured, crying like she's supplying the world with another body of water, grieving like grief is a living organism hugging her tight.

And I lunge my body down to pick her up, and she fights me at first, before her body goes limp and she screams into my shoulders and chest, her voice's vibration rattling my organs. My eyes fill fast with tears, and I blink and blink so many times, but everything's a mess and there's an entire apocalypse going on inside my chest. I'm going to split at the seams.

Is this real? This can't be real. Tears keep rolling down my face. I try to wipe them away with my arm, but they won't stop.

She's pounding on my chest as I lift her up, her face tear-streaked, eyes shut tight.

"May we come inside?" Detective Bills asks.

Mama doesn't stop wailing.

I nod, walking Mama to the kitchen table, her legs not wanting to move right.

The detectives follow us to the kitchen, glancing at each other and then at us and then back at each other. They stay quiet—real quiet.

I pull up a chair next to Mama, and the detectives sit across from us. I'm taking turns patting her on the back and wiping my face with my sleeve.

"Oh, God!" Mama wails even louder. "My baby boy!"

"I'm so sorry," Detective Bills says.

"Yes, Mrs. Johnson," Detective Parker adds. "I know this isn't the news you were hoping for, but I assure you all the details will be transparent soon. There wasn't a police report on file, but our team is gathering all the details as we speak."

This doesn't stop Mama from breaking down. And it doesn't take my heart from out of my stomach or stop me from feeling like there's a house fire inside me, burning everything to ash.

It hits me—so damn hard.

Tyler didn't even disappear. He was dead all along. And

realizing that a part of me is now gone, I can't stop shaking my head and my chest goes numb. I can't believe it. From here on out, every memory between us will be one-sided, and only I will be able to piece together all the little details, without Tyler correcting me, telling his version of them.

A lump rises in my throat. I forget how to swallow.

This ain't even fair, man.

I place my hands in front of me, looking at them and wondering why Tyler and not anyone else? Hell, why him and not me?

Detective Bills clears his throat and leans in. "We think this death was somehow linked to the gang fight that occurred on Friday, where we arrested Mr. Johntae Smith and two other minors."

Mama shakes her head, sobbing. These words bang up on one another in my head.

"Detective Bills and I could take the two of you down to identify the body right now, if you'd like, ma'am," Detective Parker says.

"I gotta see if it's real. I gotta see if it's really my baby," Mama says, her voice breaking. We all rise from the table, and my legs feel tingly and weak. The detectives open the front door, and I help Mama walk out to their black car.

The inside of the car smells like mints and coffee. Mama and I soak the black leather seats with our tears. It's so hard to breathe, but I squeeze Mama's hand and shut my eyes and try my best to allow air into my lungs.

●

The ride to the county morgue is painfully long. Mama wraps her arms around me and presses my head into her shoulder. It's soft, and I can hear her heart beating fast, no, breaking, over and over again.

When we arrive at the morgue, Detective Bills opens the door for us and Detective Parker walks us toward the building. I look up, taking tiny steps next to Mama, keeping my eyes on the brown-and-red brick building that gives me chills. Each step closer to the concrete stairs leading to the door makes something inside me tighten.

Detective Bills comes up behind me and places his hand on my back.

Walking inside, it feels like I'm stepping into a hospital, and the smell of bleach and glass cleaner hits me in the face. I expected it to smell like death—sulfur or rotten eggs. The smell of sterilization is too strong, so I cover my nose with my shirt.

We're greeted by two people in long white lab coats, Mr. Garcia and Ms. Collins. They lead us down a long hallway of doors, and we walk into a small room with three normal walls and one made of glass. It's cramped and looks like an interrogation room, four chairs around a metal table in the center.

Mama and I sit on one side.

Mr. Garcia and Ms. Collins sit on the other, pulling out manila folders and paperwork.

"Where is he? When can I see him? I need to see him," Mama says, her eyes looking up at the ceiling, lips vibrating, legs shaking.

"The body is in the other room," Mr. Garcia says.

"I need to see him," Mama says over and over again. My face feels so hot and my throat tightens.

"We don't wish to trigger any further trauma, so we give the option of showing a photograph of the body instead," Ms. Collins says.

"I want to see *him*," I blurt out, not really realizing that I even opened my mouth.

The two of them nod at each other.

"Very well," Mr. Garcia says, putting away the manila folders.

Ms. Collins murmurs, like she's trying to keep her voice down, "Mr. Garcia will show you the body and the autopsy report."

I hate how they keep saying "the body." My heart stops and then starts and then stops all over again every time they say it.

"I'm here to answer any questions you might have, and will be with you throughout the entire identification process," Mr. Garcia says. "Sound good?"

Silence washes over the room for a moment.

Mr. Garcia gets up to hold the door open for us. I'm taking so many deep breaths, and my lungs feel so damn heavy. We all file out the room, my arm interlocked with Mama's. I can feel her shaking, like she just stepped inside a freezer or something. And I'm shaking, too.

We turn and take a few steps down the hallway, and Mr. Garcia says, "Right in here."

I blink harder and slower as we enter the room. It's cold, and I can hear an unseen air-conditioning unit blasting air inside. Mr. Garcia leads us to a metal table on wheels with a blue sheet over it.

My heart pounds. I can't move. I can't breathe. I can't feel anything. Mama's eyes get real wide and she's shaking even harder now.

Mr. Garcia pulls back the blue sheet. I squeeze my eyes shut. I don't want to see. I *can't* see this.

Mama loses it. "Oh my God!" she screams, her voice splitting in so many places.

I swallow. Then, I look.

The boy on the table is Tyler—that's what my eyes tell me; that's what my brain says. Same fivehead forehead. Same nose. It's Tyler, but it's also not. His eyes are so glossy and pale, not the familiar brown I remember. His skin is different, like a plastic mannequin's that's grayer than his brown. His mouth is open, like he was letting out a final breath of air. There's dirt and grass and blood still in his hair.

My stomach twists. A sob slips out from deep within my gut.

Mama leans over Tyler's body. She doesn't touch him— just looks at him, like she's trying to press in her mind that he's really not coming back to us, or like she's trying to scrape up some hope that it's not really him.

I watch Mr. Garcia walk over to the other side of the room and grab a clipboard. He comes back and writes something down. "Is this Tyler Johnson?"

I can't even nod right now.

Mama says, "That's my son," and I feel the whole world shake inside me.

Mr. Garcia begins to read the autopsy report. "There are three holes in the body. One in the chest, near the heart. Two in the stomach area. We found three bullets belonging to a Glock 22 lodged inside."

My mouth goes numb.

I'm going to be sick or faint or both.

I run out the room, not even looking back. As soon as I get outside, I'm throwing up all over the steps. Everything

I've eaten is coming out my mouth and it's like every drop of water in my body pours from my eyes.

I wipe my mouth with my sleeve. My chest fucking hurts.

And I feel like I'm dying.

•

The detectives drive Mama and me back home, and the two of us have finally gone a whole five minutes without busting out into tears. We just sit on the couch, staring straight ahead, lights off and curled up into each other, like how we'd do when I was a little kid and Tyler and I would take naps with her.

Everything inside me feels emptied out. And I don't know what to do. I can't think about anything, and I don't want to think about him being gone. I would be okay if the two of us stayed like this forever.

· 16 ·

The next day, Mama stays in her bedroom, the door closed but not blocking out the sound of her crying. I sit alone in the living room, staring at the TV but not really watching it, trying to distract myself from my new reality. This reality—where I'm alive and my brother is not.

I text G-mo and Ivy to tell them what happened, and they come over a couple hours before school even lets out, catching me by surprise, tears streaming down their faces, hands shaking, and it almost seems like they're trying so hard not to look me in the eyes.

And as if words are the hardest things in the universe, Ivy stutters, "Th-th-there's a v-v-video that leaked online."

"A video?" This can't be real. And I feel like the smallest thing in the room.

"Some anonymous account posted it. It's everywhere, man," G-mo adds. And he asks me for my phone.

I try to ignore that it's the same phone I shared with Tyler as I hand it to him, my heart rate picking up. I sit back down on the couch.

He returns the phone to me and then places a hand on my shoulder, leaving it for a while. "We thought you'd want to see it, too."

G-mo and Ivy sit across from me. Maybe it's all in my head, but our living room seems to be closing in on us.

I mute the TV and hold up the phone to see the footage for myself.

I press play.

I can see him: It's night, and there's Tyler, walking beneath a streetlight so bright it might as well be day, his hands in the air. I hear my brother's voice. He's saying over and over again: "Leave me alone. I'm just going home." There's a cop in his uniform, his back to the camera. Tyler turns to him. My brother's face, my brother's body—alive. He pushes the cop away. And then the *pop* of a gun. *Pop. Pop.* The camera tilts and goes completely black.

I hear the shots replay on loop.

Pop! One.

I fight for breath.

Pop! Two.

I'm about to black out.

Pop! Three.

No, no, no, no, no. This. Can't. Be. Real.

I stare at the dark phone screen. And then my chest expands and retracts fast, my throat drying, a lump burning up in my gut.

"That's not him," I say through tears, the words falling out all jumbled and wet. "It can't be." I want the world to swallow me up. And it sinks in, kind of like how all the sand sinks to the bottom of an hourglass.

Tyler is gone.

I'm just going home. My brother's last words echo in my head as I shudder, mostly out of fear and so much damn misery. I could vomit right now. My stomach folds from my racing thoughts.

I'm going to be sick. All of my breath leaves my body. And suddenly, I can't be in this room anymore.

I storm outside, hop on my bike, and ride away as fast as I can. I don't have a destination in mind. I just need to get away. I need to go somewhere I don't have to think about what I just watched, where I don't have to think about how my own brother died at the hands of a police officer, where I don't have to think about a world without Tyler.

I need a safe place. The tears keep coming before I can stop them, drying on my chin as huge gusts of wind come over me. I let the world distort around me until I'm slamming my bike down in front of Faith's place. There're two cars in the driveway, so I know she's not alone. But I don't care. I need to be with her.

I knock on the door, hands shaking. My head feels heavy, and my throat is so dry it's like I've eaten an entire box of saltines.

I clutch my elbows, waiting for her to answer, spilling my tears on her porch.

Faith opens the door. "Marvin. Oh my God. Are you okay?"

She lets me in, and I sit on the couch and tell her everything. It takes so long for the words to come out between my sobs, but she's patient and keeps her hand on my back, rubbing it slowly. I show her the video and she flinches and says, "What the hell?"

Before I know it, there's a set of brown eyes and long eyelashes in front of me. It's Faith's mama. She puts her hands on my back, telling me, "Let it out, honey. Let it all out, honey." She doesn't even know me, but I don't care and she doesn't either.

"I just don't know what to do," I keep saying over and over. The video is stained in my mind, playing over and over again. I shut my eyes tight, trying to shake the footage out of my head, but I can't. I just fucking can't.

Pop! One.

I shake my head hard.

Pop! Two.

I imagine Tyler's final gasp of oxygen.

Pop! Three.

I'm suddenly throwing up in a small trash can. I'm powerless and I have no control over my own brain or stomach. I don't move. I can't. I just cry, throw up, cry, and throw up again.

Faith puts a hand on my arm. "Hey, I'm so sorry." I look up at her and see she's crying, too.

She hugs me.

I hug her back and let out a slight breath.

Faith's mama offers me some hot tea. I tell her no, thank you.

She gives me a regretful face, opens her mouth, and keeps it open for a little while. Then she says in a sympathetic voice, "I'm sorry for your loss. The man who did this to your brother is going to be punished." I think this was supposed to be a way to reassure me or something, but I only feel stunned.

I don't even feel like being.

As I keep my head in my hands, Faith and her mama take turns trying to comfort me. "There'll be justice for y'all," her mom says. "You have all my empathy."

But I don't even deserve empathy. If anybody does, it's Mama.

Part of me regrets leaving Mama alone. I wasn't thinking when I left. She needs me, and I need her—now more than ever.

I leave Faith's house, and as I ride back under a fading, starry sky, my stomach feels like a churning abyss, and I hurt too much not to start tearing up.

At home, G-mo and Ivy are still at my place. Mama's come out of her room, and I take one look at her, and I can tell she's seen the video, too. The TV is on with the volume down low, and on the news I can see images of the video that captured the last minute of my brother's life. Tyler Johnson has become breaking news, and I feel raw and pissed off that the last few seconds of his life and his death are on display for the whole fucking world to see. He wouldn't have wanted that.

There're Chinese food cartons scattered across the coffee table, the smell of soy sauce and fried rice reminding me that I'm hungry and that I still have to eat because I'm alive, even if Tyler is not.

"Hey, Marvin," G-mo says. He's standing next to Mama. She's still and quiet, just staring forward.

I nod at him and walk over to Mama. I pat her on the back, doing my best not to have a breakdown again. There's so much I want to say and so much static in my brain, and I can't find a way to say it. I just keep rubbing her back.

Ivy's lying on the floor, going through a photo book Mama put together last night, showing me some of her favorites.

Ivy points to this one picture of Tyler and me when we were little, playing cops and robbers with Dad. The two of us are in tank tops and shorts. In the picture, Tyler and I are each holding a water gun, and Dad's chasing us.

Ripples of nausea and ache creep up on me.

And I don't know when the pain is going to end.

After G-mo and Ivy leave, Mama and I remain a mess in the living room. Mama calls Detective Conaway and asks him if they're going to get the man who did it, if they're locking him up. They talk about the video and about Tyler and about the investigation and about standard procedure, but Mama doesn't take their mess. She stays on the phone for hours, and after she hangs up, all frustrated and broken, she decides that she needs to be alone in her room again.

●

I open up the video while lying in bed, and I'm not even sure why. Each time I watch it, I feel like someone is surgically ripping out all of my insides without any anesthetic. It's as if I notice something new—something fucking worse—the more I see and hear it. I don't really know why the news keeps calling it an event, an altercation. I've never heard murder pronounced that way. What happened wasn't just an altercation. It was fucking slaughter, man. The officer's name is everywhere: Thomas Meredith. I feel sick.

When I click off the video, I try my best to stop myself from scrolling through the hashtags—to keep from diving headfirst into such a shallow pool of hatred—because I know there'll only be white people waiting on me, wanting to try to hold me under the water until I go silent, waiting until I'm in total fear of blue and white. But after the tenth time of playing it, I have to take a break, before I fucking die from brokenness and rage.

I close the video and scroll through my timeline.

All I see are hashtags floating around: #PrayersForTyler-Johnson and #EndPoliceBrutality, and oppressive ones, like #BlueLivesMatter.

Clicking on each brings up a slew of posts. Photos. Videos of people speaking out on their own phones. Links to similar cases. It's all so overwhelming.

I'm seeing so many All Lives Matter bullshit posts that have my entire body shaking. People don't fucking know that black folks were never included in the *All*. *All-American* means white. *All-inclusive* means white. *All lives* means white lives. It's bullshit. White folks always make it about them, and I'm pissed off that they're trying to mask their hatred with these tags.

But the craziest thing to see is all the pictures snatched from Tyler's social media pages—pictures that even I haven't seen before. Some of them are of him dressed in a black suit and tie; some are of him in his everyday wear: dark jeans and a hoodie. Others are close-ups of his face, as if they're mug shots, even though he's never been arrested once. People are saying that my father was a criminal and a monster, so Tyler had it coming. I guess that's the most fucked-up part of all the social media bullshit.

I scroll through the comments.

Maybe if he wasn't holding a bag of dope, he'd be alive.

Fuck black people. #WhiteLivesMatter

He looks like he'd rob a store.

What did you people want? To give him a freebie to commit a crime cause he's black? He was a bad dude.

Tyler ≠ a bad dude.

Tyler = bright and loving.

Tyler = my brother, who was killed.

There are also comments and replies to posts that are lighter and just more, uh, human, and I don't fucking know why, but they still hurt.

Tyler, you're in a better place. Heaven ain't racist.

This kid was a fucking Basketball prodigy! I'll miss playing after school with him. #RIPBro

You deserved better than this. Your family is in my prayers. Always.

Everything in the world is just a divided and blurry mess. The real world. The online one. All of it has just become too fucked up for me to even feel human. The more I scroll and see all the photos and hashtags, the more I feel monstrous.

It gets to the point where even the hurt fucking hurts.

I try to sleep, but I can't even get my eyes to close. I'm lying on a soft mattress, eyes wide, and Tyler's somewhere in the morgue.

· 17 ·

I really want to just stay home and lie in bed and watch episodes of *A Different World* on Netflix and block the world out, but I can't—and I don't. A part of me hopes that Sojo High will help clear and ease my mind.

I'm hoping for a distraction.

I don't want to look at my phone.

G-mo and Ivy meet at my house to walk with me to school. Ivy's eating an Oatmeal Creme Pie. I remember debating about them with Tyler. He thought Fudge Rounds were better. He always had bad taste. My chest gets tight.

When I walk through the doors of Sojo High, people do one of those Red Sea splits like I'm Moses or some shit, and everyone's staring at us up and down, whispering to one another.

"Mr. Johnson." Principal Dodson stops me as I'm walking to my locker.

I turn around, shrugging my shoulders. "What?" And it comes out a bit ruder than I meant, but it's too late to take it back, and besides, Dodson's a dick. And I don't even feel like talking right now.

He walks up to me, angry-eyed and flustered, gripping a coffee mug in his hand. "Are you ready for today?" His nose is pointed up, flaring.

I almost talk myself out of it, but I reply like a decent human being would. "Yeah, as ready as I can be, emotionally and all." My gaze drops to the floor.

"Very good. Carry on, Mr. Johnson."

●

In first-period English class, Ms. Tanner goes easy on us, and we discuss, as a class, the themes and motifs in *Antigone* and *Oedipus the King*.

But Tyler.

My twin is gone.

"Guillermo," Ms. Tanner says, pointing at him as he dozes off. "Please write a theme on the board."

G-mo takes his precious time getting up there. He uses an orange Expo marker, so light that it's hard to see. *Power*, he writes in big, bubbly, graffiti-like letters.

Ms. Tanner calls on a new girl who started a few weeks ago. She writes *The role of women* on the board in curly letters.

"Mr. Johnson," Ms. Tanner says with a smile. "Would you like to finish our list off?"

And I inhale, getting out of my seat. Hands shaking, I write in black marker a few more themes that come to mind. *Determination. Greed. Hate. Mortality. Fate.*

It's like Antigone and I are one and the same. It's like the themes of her story are the same themes in mine. I stand at the front of the classroom for several agonizing seconds, everyone staring at me.

I sit back down, all eyes on me like I've suddenly become the most popular dude in school because of what happened to my brother.

"These themes are all important and relevant to your lives," Ms. Tanner says, walking to the front of the room and underlining each theme as she speaks. "Power, greed, hate, determination, fate and free will, mortality—these are all things that you see in your community around you. We live in a society where attaining power is of the utmost importance, resulting in greed for very many of us." She walks to stand next to her desk and leans against the surface. "Some of us, unfortunately, learn the hard way about the tension between individual action and fate. Like Antigone." She pauses before she walks back to the board and circles tonight's homework.

The bell rings. I can finally exhale.

I run out of class, not saying anything to anyone.

It's time for my interview with an MIT representative, and already I know that it isn't going to go well. I forgot to "dress for success," like I want to really be somebody someday. And I'm going to be late.

· 18 ·

'm a total of two minutes late to my interview in room
B252, a biology lab around the corner from the media
center. In the hallway, I pass booths of local community
colleges and other universities—random and faraway ones,
like the University of Chicago, Florida State University, Cor-
nell, and a bunch of others—each a part of the college fair.
They've got flags and banners and balloons and little sign-up
sheets.

I round the corner and walk into room B252, and suddenly I'm taking a step into what could be my future, what

could be my way out of the cycle—a step that Tyler never got to take.

My heart pounds like it's drumming the MIT fight song to get me ready. And I can taste the anxiety on my tongue as I stare into the face of a light-skinned man with grayish hair. I can already tell this is going to be messy.

"Oh, hello! I'm Dave Ross. Are you Mr. Marvin…uh… Johnson?" the man says, standing up and smiling hugely, like he's shocked to see a black boy walking into the room.

We shake hands. "Yes, I am." There's a short pause before we sit simultaneously.

The man shuffles through a large stack of papers in front of him. "I can't seem to find your application," he says finally, organizing the stack again.

I flinch. "Oh, I'm sorry, sir. I meant to send the application in early, before the college fair, but I didn't end up having a chance."

"Young man, MIT is looking for students who are goal-oriented and want to be there and nowhere else. We expect to sit down with students who are truly committed to their futures."

I nod, looking away from him, wanting to explain everything that's been happening, but I don't. And I can feel the sweat forming all over my body in hidden crevices.

"So, what makes you an MIT man?" he says, skepticism creeping into his voice.

"I don't know, sir. It's just been a dream of mine to get into MIT, change the world, show people what I can achieve. Sometimes it feels like people don't think I can achieve anything, and I want to prove them wrong."

He runs a hand through his scruffy hair, frowning. "If I had a dime for every time someone gave me that answer, I'd have a year's salary."

I pause, feeling my heart sink, the sting of defeat pinching me.

"Let's rephrase the question. What do you want out of MIT?"

"A decent education." My shoulders shrug.

"You can get that at a lot of schools." He pauses, tilting his glasses down from his face a little. "So, why MIT?"

I blink, feeling beads of sweat on my forehead. My back sticks to the chair like a wet page.

"Sir, MIT is all I've ever wanted," I say. "Since I was in the fourth grade, I knew that I wanted to be at this school. I knew I wanted to be someplace where I'd defy all the odds, where I'd grow and become a better person, where I'd get one of the finest educations this country has to offer."

"Now, that's more of an answer for us, Mr. Johnson." He

nods slowly, marking down notes. "What do your parents think of your dream of attending MIT?"

My tongue presses up against my cheek, and I look at the ceiling, thinking about Principal Dodson telling me not to embarrass him. I tell him the truth. "Dad is in jail for a crime he didn't commit, because our justice system is corrupt, and sometimes it feels like I don't even have a dad anymore because of that."

I watch his eyebrows furrow and he gives me a side-smile, like he feels sorry for me.

"What about your mother?"

"Mama doesn't know much about this interview," I answer him. Really, she doesn't know about it, period.

"Why?" He leans back, chewing on the cap of his pen. "Why doesn't your mother know?"

"Her mind is somewhere else." I sigh. And now I'm realizing that mine is also.

"Where, Mr. Johnson? Where *is* her mind? Is it drugs?"

I sort of roll my eyes, a bad taste in my mouth. "No. Sir." My chest feels tight, my throat is numb, and it's so fucking hard to breathe right now.

"Then what is it, Mr. Johnson?" He squints at me, a small frown that passes quickly. I close my eyes for a few seconds, inhaling and exhaling hard.

I see Tyler lying on that metal table. The video plays back

in my head. Tyler's voice swishes around the room like the blood in my veins, and I squeeze my eyes shut.

Pop!

Pop!

Pop!

I blink back the tears.

"Her mind is on my brother. He die—no—he was murdered," I say.

"I'm so sorry to hear that, Mr. Johnson." Silence takes over the room again.

I nod, trying so hard to ignore the sourness in my stomach.

"Your brother is dead, and you're here?" He closes his files and points at me with his pen. "That says a lot about your character, Mr. Johnson. Very courageous of you."

Fuck that. Fuck courage. Fuck it all. And now I feel so shitty because he's right. I'm here in a fucking interview and my brother is fucking dead.

"Would you like to reschedule the interview? For an African-American male with your record—strong grades, glowing recommendations, and nearly perfect SAT scores—I'd love to give this a second chance. We need more students like you, Mr. Johnson."

I try to ignore his you-are-smart-for-a-black-kid suggestion. "Maybe this isn't a good idea after all."

He leans back in his seat. "I see. How about this?" He

drops his pen on the desk in front of him. "The first part of the application is due January first. How about you send your application in, and if everything is as impressive as we've been led to expect, I'll be happy to recommend you. I wouldn't normally tell a student that before seeing his formal application, but I think you're potentially the right fit for MIT, and you'd help diversify our student body. How does that sound?"

I brush my face with the palms of my hands, feeling my eyes blink one, two, three times. "Yes, I'll have it ready by then." My heart thuds and my ears ring, but there's a blanket of calmness that suddenly wraps around me.

"Very well, Mr. Johnson." We shake hands again.

As I leave the room, my phone buzzes in my pocket.

I silently wish for it to be Mama, or maybe Ivy and G-mo asking how everything went down with my interview, but it's just a Twitter notification that Faith is now following me.

· 19 ·

DATE: NOVEMBER 16, 2018

TO: MARVIN D. JOHNSON (MY SON)
FROM: JAMAL P. JOHNSON
PRISON NUMBER: 2076-14-5555
MESSAGE:
Son,
   I don't have the words to express my
pain. I know it's a pain you're feeling, too.

People will try to convince you that you don't deserve to live.

That you don't deserve to exist.

They'll ignore your voice. Lock you up.

They'll even kill you to take you out of this world.

And through it all, you have to fight. Fight to remind yourself that you do matter. That you do deserve to exist. That you do deserve to have your voice heard.

When the whole world's trying to convince you that you don't matter, it can be a constant struggle—day in, day out—to remember that you do.

But you have to. Because if you don't, then that's really when you've lost yourself.

Tyler is gone, and as his and your father I should've been there, should've protected him. I'm sorry, Marvin. But I want to do better by you.

I know you're feeling anger. You're feeling hatred for the man who took Tyler away from us. But don't let that

anger and hatred consume you, or that
man's taken your life, too.
I love you.
      Stay strong,
      Daddy

If you have a brother, and he dies, what do you do? Do you suddenly stop saying that you have one? Do you pretend he was just a piece of your past that you'll slowly start to forget?

I remember the huge protests after other shootings of black and brown kids. I need to do that, too. I need to make people aware of what happened to Tyler. I have to lift my voice, and I can't keep being quiet, sitting around as if I'm waiting for things to fix themselves.

I stay home to be with Mama the next day, laptop turned away so that she doesn't know I'm scrolling through pages and pages of Google searches on how to begin protests. I can't just sit at home and cry and grieve because that ain't going to do shit, and it ain't going to bring Tyler back either.

Mama gets up to go into her room, but I barely look away from the laptop. The sites provide lots of advice, like to have a goal in mind, and to choose a time and location that will work for the most people, and to remember that even if someone tries to shut it down, my voice deserves to be heard just as much as anyone else's. Some sites say I need permits to start a protest, but permits don't always get approved. The most important part of planning a protest is making sure people know about it. Some of the biggest protests took off because word spread through social media, like Twitter and Facebook and Tumblr.

I spend most of my day looking up the most successful protests, like the 2011 Egyptian revolution, and the Black Lives Matter protests, too. And after hours of searching through sites on protests, I find contact information for a man named Albert Sharp. He coordinates protests right here in Sterling Point for civil liberties and unjust events, like the killing of my brother. I send him an e-mail. He's the perfect person to help me plan the protest that Tyler deserves. My blood runs hot just thinking about it.

●

Ivy and G-mo stop over after school. They come bringing me Hot Fries and peanut butter M&M's and stories about all the mess going around—mess ranging from general high school drama to people spreading lies about Tyler, like how he was a gangbanging thug.

I squeeze my eyes shut and practice breathing in and out.

"How'd you sleep?" Ivy asks me, breaking the quiet.

"Fine," I lie. I couldn't sleep last night. Something in my

head, in my chest, in my stomach refused to shut off and allow me to fucking sleep. The whole night I just stared at the cloak-like darkness of my ceiling, hoping to at least feel Tyler's presence.

My mind replays the video of Tyler's murder—over and over again.

Pop! Pop! Pop! Man, I'm losing it.

Ivy takes my hand. "You don't need to lie—not to us, Marvin."

I tear up. The air's burning my skin. I take my hand away, wipe my eyes. "I'm just sick of sitting here and not doing anything."

G-mo raises his eyebrows. "What would you do?"

"I don't know. I've been looking up ways to protest. And there's this guy, Albert Sharp. I don't know."

We sit there for a while, and Mama comes out of her room. She doesn't say anything, just shuffles into the living room, her hair a mess and dark circles around her eyes. Ivy and G-mo greet her, but she doesn't say anything—just fiddles with a cigarette and a lighter, struggling to get it lit. I look at Mama and my heart breaks all over again, because I don't think I'm looking at her—not really. I'm looking at a shadow of her, since the real Mama is gone, just like Tyler.

But I can't lose myself, too. I have to focus on getting him justice. Letting the whole world know that he was murdered.

Having the whole world screaming his name. That's what Tyler deserves. That's what Tyler would want.

Mama sits down beside me on the couch.

Something's pulling at my lungs. And my throat feels like it's getting tight.

Shit. Shit. Shit. I lay my hands out in my lap and put my head down.

"He's fucking gone," I mumble, my voice cracking.

Mama's shadow grips my hand, squeezing tight as if she's trying to tell me something without using words, like *We're in this together.* Like she's trying to bring herself back into this life.

A breaking news alert flashes red on the TV with the caption STERLING POINT OFFICER ARRESTED FOR THE DEATH OF TYLER JOHNSON.

"Finally" is all Mama says, and it comes out in a really hopeful breath. "All I want is for that man to pay for what he did."

A picture of the officer's face flashes across the screen. He has chilling blue eyes and balding blond hair and a yellow mustache. I know he'll be seared into my memory as the man who took my brother away from me. The man who looked at my brother, a living person, a working body, an actual soul, and decided to take him out of this world because of his own hatred, his own darkness. I don't want to look at that man's face on the TV screen, because if I do, I think I'll scream and cry and throw up all at the same time. But I can't let myself look away. I have to look evil in the eye—have to face him, the way Tyler did. This man's face was the last he saw. I try not to imagine what that must've been like for him—the pain of bullets ripping through his body, the shock as he hit the ground, and the only other person with him is this man, his killer.

And I'm feeling really conflicted right now. This sort of thing happens too often. Innocent people getting killed by the cops. I've heard it so many times. No indictments. No convictions. No punishment at all. I mean, this is a step in the right direction, and I should be happy, right? They're treating this officer's actions as a crime. But for now at least, he's still alive, and that's more than what can be said for Tyler.

Ivy and G-mo exchange looks, and Ivy keeps shaking her head, like they're having a telepathic conversation.

"What?" I say. "What's going on?"

Ivy lets out a breath, and G-mo leans forward in his seat. "There's been anger, you know, for what happened," he says.

"Just say it, man."

He sucks in air. "Well, some people are angry that there's anger."

I squint at him. "What do you mean?"

Mama just sucks on her cigarette, staring at the TV.

G-mo licks his lips. "See for yourself. It's all over Twitter."

I pull out the phone I shared with Tyler and scroll through my Twitter feed until I find what they're talking about. Tweets that go beyond saying Tyler's a gangbanging thug. Tweets that take it too fucking far. Tweets that say he deserved what he got. Shit about police having the right to protect themselves. I scroll until I see a video with a kid from school—some white guy named Lance Anderson, a senior at Sojo High. He and some other random kids with matching plain white shirts talk into the camera, saying how it's such a shame that the cops are being punished for doing something real good for the city. He's called for a protest in defense of the cop who murdered my brother; it's going to happen on Christmas Day.

I give Ivy, who's across from me, a look, and then I glance at G-mo, feeling my heart beat hard inside my chest—so hard, because there's never just enough with these white people. Racists like this dude always find a way to make matters worse, find ways to justify hate. We never gave them a reason to hate us. But they don't even care about that. They're so fragile and afraid of people who are different that they have to give so much hate to others just to feel big, just to feel alive.

"I'm sorry you had to see that," Ivy says quietly.

G-mo gives me this tight-lipped frown and glances at

the TV and then back at me, his eyes wide and infuriated. "What the literal fuck is going on? Are people seriously this ignorant? Lance can't actually be this motherfucking stupid, can he? Sorry for the language, Mrs. Johnson."

My jaw tightens and my heart pounds.

Breathe, Marvin. Just keep breathing. In. Out. In. Out.

Ivy looks as if she's still processing all of this. Her fists are clenched at her sides, like she's ready to punch a hole straight through the dude's face.

"Why don't some white people want to acknowledge police brutality?" I ask, feeling like the world has just used me to wipe its ass. "Why don't they care about us?"

"Some won't even say the words 'police brutality,' bro," Ivy says.

I shake my head. Mama stands up from the couch and gets Auntie Nicola on the phone. I can hear her voice as she sits in the kitchen—can hear as she begins to sob, which puts an aching in my chest.

I want one more chance to talk to Tyler—to see his smile, to hear his laugh, to save him, to tell him how he was always the better part of the equation.

I remember when Mama made Tyler and me go to Bible school on Sundays. The Sunday school teacher kept calling Tyler a prophet, saying one day he would grow up to be a teacher of the word of God himself, that he'd recruit more believers. I remember Tyler going around school bragging about what the teacher told him.

And I smile. And my eyes water. And I fucking hurt.

G-mo and Ivy stay as long as they can, until their curfews, and then they bike and skate home when they have to.

When I get in my bed, I text Faith, telling her about how I can't ignore this huge gaping hole that's consuming me every single second of every single day. She texts back, saying she's going to pick me up.

●

Faith pulls to a stop in front of my house after I sneak out my window. The car ride is silent for the most part, which I really fucking need right now. At least for a little while longer.

We ride past a series of abandoned buildings, all rusted and covered in vines and weeds—graffitied up and sad, leaning back a little, like the construction of the hood wants to take a step away from itself, travel back a couple decades in history.

Everything about this place looks uglier up close, when you really see it for what it is and not what it used to be. Especially at night, when everything is just washed in darkness and violence—so brutal and so shallow. Groups of boys wearing all black huddle around fire hydrants—not because they are curious as to what would happen if they were to open it, but because the tip of the hydrant is a great place to set a dime bag and lethal weapons for intimidation. And I make a mental promise to myself that one day I'll really make it out of here. I *need* to make it out of here.

"Thanks for the ride," I mumble. My voice sounds dry and raspy.

"It's cool," she answers, stopping at a red light. And she just nods at the road in front of her, flipping hair out of her brown face. And I get chills. I'm left telling myself that I shouldn't even be getting chills right now. I feel guilty, looking at Faith and feeling the way I do about her when my brother is dead.

I gaze back out the window at the constellations, but they have me feeling more boxed-in and trapped, reminding me I've got a bunch of tunnels of darkness to walk through, because I was born into this skin, this hood, this fate. And I'm quiet, wondering how I go on from here.

She clears her throat and rolls down the window to let some air in. "You know my heart is bleeding right now, right? I'm so sorry," she says, but it's like it's physically uncomfortable for her to say the words, like she's suddenly remembering all the people she's lost in her own life at once. "And I hope the man who did it gets put away for life."

"Me too," I say, staring into her eyes.

"Will there be a funeral for Tyler?" she asks, and inhales deeply from the crack in her window, continuing down some dark street.

"I don't know. I don't think so. Mama hasn't said anything about it. Besides, we don't have very much family, so it would just be the two of us and Auntie Nicola anyway. Money's also pretty tight around the house." But just the thought of a funeral for Tyler has my heart in my stomach. How does someone go about doing something like that anyway? Like, how could you plan to put your brother in a box to be stuffed in the ground forever?

Faith asks me about my folks and about how Tyler and I grew up. And I tell her everything, which makes me sound like I'm the epitome of the stereotype for black boys. Dad in jail. Mama worked hard to keep the family stable, raising two boys—playing the role of Mama and Papa. And I tell her that Tyler and I grew up like peas in a pod. For years, we were squeezed together, side by side, knowing each other through and through, playing basketball in the streets and NBA 2K on the weekends when shit went down, and then one day our roots split from our pod and we slowly started growing in different directions.

"One time, Tyler and I made a bet on Super Bowl Forty-Seven. Forty-Niners versus the Ravens. I was for the Ravens and he was for the Forty-Niners. When the Ravens won, he got so mad because he had to give me five dollars." I press down a small laugh.

"Oh yeah?" She flashes me a smile.

"We didn't talk for a week," I say, and it hits me that I'll never get to talk to him again.

There actually were a zillion things I could have said to him that final moment at the party. I didn't know how. I didn't know how to tell my brother that I was afraid we were going in two separate directions, that I was scared I'd lose him forever. And now it's too late. I'll have to live with that.

She gives me this sad look. "You blame yourself, don't you?"

For a moment, I struggle to respond. I do—I blame myself for not being there enough for Tyler when he needed me. I blame myself for saying all the wrong things and doing all the wrong things. I blame myself for letting him hang around Johntae's crew.

If only I could have stopped everything. Suddenly, the image of Tyler shot dead on the ground, blood pouring out of him, his cold body all alone and abandoned, takes control of my thoughts. I blink hard, trying to flash the image away, my fists balling up at my sides.

I nod and gulp my answer to her, like a baby trying to utter its first word. When she cuts off the car and pulls the key out of the ignition, I come crashing back to reality.

"I just don't want to believe it. I just don't know what's real."

"You loved him, and I'm sure he loved you. That was real—and that's all that matters," she says.

Fuck, man, I feel tears coming up.

"It hurts, Faith," I say. "I'll never get to see my brother alive again."

Dammit. A few seconds slip by, and I stare at her Betty Boop floor mat on the passenger side, wetness on my face.

I look up and realize that we're at some fancy-looking building that definitely isn't a part of Sterling Point.

"Where are we?"

"This is my dad's law firm," she says. "I've never met him, but this is where I came when my best friend, Kayla, got killed in a drive-by."

I wipe underneath my eyes, scanning the building.

"I went all the way to the roof and overlooked the town. I thought about jumping right then," she says. "I looked up and it was like I heard her telling me that she'd come back and slap the shit out of me if I jumped." She laughs.

I'm so glad she didn't. I'm glad she stayed. But I'm feeling like I want to jump myself right now.

She reaches for my hand. "My point is that I know what you're feeling inside. I know that ache inside your heart. And I'm living proof that losing a loved one doesn't stop you from beating yourself, blaming yourself, wanting to die yourself, but Kayla is in me as much as Tyler is in you. They'd want us to fight, not surrender."

I look into her brown eyes. "Yeah. You're right."

She gives me this side-smile that makes me want to smile back.

●

Eventually, she starts the car again and we get moving, just enjoying each other's company, moving at forty-five miles per hour through the empty streets, talking about how the best way to make sure Tyler gets justice—the best way to make sure I do right by him one more time—is to take the fight inside me to the streets. We have to demand it. We have to do everything within our power to raise our voices. We have to protest. Just praying and hoping for justice and grace and mercy won't help us right now.

Faith tells me that Frederick Douglass said, "I prayed for twenty years. Nothing happened until I got off my knees and started marching with my feet."

●

Faith drops me back off at my place. I get in bed and stare at my ceiling, thinking about Tyler's cold, lifeless body, damaged and barely recognizable, and I put a pillow over my face and scream and cry into it as loud as I can.

It's the thought of living a life of fear that takes me back to the day Dad was dragged away. I'd started having trouble sleeping because I was afraid there were monsters in my room, hiding under my bed and waiting for me in my closet. The monsters cast their big-ass silhouettes along my walls, creating shapes that made me feel small.

One night, as sirens blared and gunpowder rained down outside my cracked window, I called out for someone— maybe Mama—to come and fight away the monsters in the dark. But when I called, Tyler came instead of Mama.

He walked in and sat on the edge of my bed, a worried look in his eyes, like he, too, felt uneasy at the sound of sirens. Like he, too, could see the monsters. He checked under my bed to soothe my fears.

And all of a sudden, I'm really fucking hating Marvin Johnson, because I could never be like Tyler, could never be as brave as him, could never soothe his fears. I couldn't even fucking be there for him when he needed me most.

And I'm reminded of three things: 1) I'm a complete fuckup; 2) monsters can appear in broad daylight; and 3) Tyler will never again physically be here.

We were born together. He wasn't supposed to die without me. And he wasn't supposed to go out like he did.

●

Despite my unwillingness, a couple more days squeeze on by anyway. I spend each day pacing back and forth throughout my house, sitting in silence, refusing all food, and repeating this over and over again.

I'm mid-pace in the living room when the six o'clock news comes on, and I see my brother's name flash in big red letters again.

I call out to Mama, who's in the bathroom with the door locked, probably just sitting on the toilet seat with the lid down like she has been for most of the day, sobbing and sniffling into a roll of toilet paper. She runs out and sits down next to me with the toilet paper in her hands; it's all wet-looking and shredded in random places. She's wearing a silky white blouse. Her hair is pulled back, straight, strands tucked behind her ears. She looks like she'll be going to Tyler's funeral for the rest of her life.

The news reporter is talking about the hearing. This hearing is crucial, Mama tells me, and will determine whether or not we get justice. But this hearing isn't going to bring Tyler back, so I don't care as much as Mama does. Mama and I exchange glances before returning to the TV screen.

And I'm left thinking to myself that this is a huge change for her. Yesterday, she signed the papers to have Tyler turned into ashes and placed in a silver urn so she wouldn't have to put him in the ground, so he could come back home one final time, and she was a turbulent hurricane of emotions, like no one would ever really understand how much she's hurting. And I couldn't really feel all the emptiness, because I did not allow myself to.

I don't think you can ever quite fill the emptiness of something you lost that was everything, everything to you. The hurt still keeps on.

Breathe in. Breathe out.

Focus. Focus on what Tyler needs: justice. The whole world screaming his name, knowing that he was here— knowing that he mattered.

I grab my laptop and scroll through Albert Sharp's website. He hasn't responded to my e-mail yet, but even if he doesn't, I know what to do. Decide on a place, decide on a time, send out a message over social media. I know that G-mo and Ivy and Faith will help spread the word. I know they'll help me make sure no one forgets my brother.

· **20** ·

At Sojo High, I'm no longer the boy whose brother went missing. I'm now the boy whose brother got himself killed. I have to tell way too many people that Tyler did not get himself killed for holding drugs for someone or for whatever the fuck they think, and that he was brutalized and killed by a cop—not because Tyler was doing anything wrong, but because the officer saw my brother as a threat just because of the color of his skin. I don't know what was going through the cop's head. But I sure as hell know that Tyler was just trying to go home.

Ms. Tanner finds me in the hallway and tells me that the principal wants to see me in his office. She makes her next class wait just so she can escort me down. *Man, this is some whack shit. I don't feel like talking to anybody, but especially not Dickface Dodson.*

On the way, she says in her usual sweet tone, "If you ever need anything, remember that I'm here." She continues with a small, bittersweet smile, telling me that she hates how the world fuels so much hatred; she hates how she can't do anything to bring Tyler back to me.

I shrug my shoulders. She has these big eyes that are filled with sympathy. And it makes me feel some type of way, like she's saying these things only to feel better about herself, as if she's trying to show me that she's not a racist, unlike Tyler's killer. I don't really want to hear it right now, but I don't want to be shitty either.

So I nod and shrug again. "Thanks, Ms. Tanner."

She folds her hands in front of her once we stop at Principal Dodson's door.

I hear him talking to someone. I can see two shadows through the matte window.

I knock twice on the door.

Dodson's muffled voice groans, "Come in."

I look back as Ms. Tanner walks to her room, heels

clicking down the long hallway, and I breathe out. I wish more teachers were as kind as her.

My stomach suddenly ties in knots, and I open the door. I see Principal Dodson standing over his desk and the MIT interviewer sitting in a chair on the other side of his office.

"Mr. Johnson, come in," both of them say in different tones. I can hear the excitement in Mr. Ross's voice and the dread in Dodson's.

I take a seat, and everything spins.

"We'll make this quick, since you have class," Principal Dodson says while exhaling, his eye twitching. "A Sojo High education is a very precious one."

And I really want to grunt something sarcastic back, but the interviewer clears his throat and extends his hand for me to shake.

"Great to see you again, Mr. Johnson," he says.

"You too," I reply, shaking his sweaty, warm hand.

"Mr. Ross from MIT is here to check in on your application, and to see if you still have interest in MIT."

"You're a very popular young man these days," Mr. Ross says. He clears his throat. "I'm sorry for your loss, Marvin."

It hurts. I don't want to be popular—not for the reasons I am. "Thank you, Mr. Ross."

"There're quite a few people at MIT who would like to have you strongly considered, given your background, your twin brother's tragedy—and your excellent test scores. It's all a great story. It's almost...symbolic, wouldn't you say?"

I have no fucking idea what he's talking about. "Yeah. Sure. Symbolic."

Mr. Dodson sits and leans forward. "But I was just explaining to Mr. Ross that you no longer have interest in attending MIT—isn't that right? Especially after your involvement with Mr. Johntae Smith's party." Principal Dodson stares coldly, like he'll hurt me—or worse, murder me—if I don't agree with him.

I turn away from him to face Mr. Ross. "I'm still interested, sir." And then a lie slips in: "I had no *involvement*, sir—I was just at the wrong place at the wrong time, and my application is coming right along."

Mr. Ross perks up and puts his files back in his attaché case. "Excellent, that's all I wanted to hear. You don't seem to respond to e-mails." He sort of laughs, adjusting his blazer.

"Yeah," I lie, "broken computer, and my neighborhood barely gets Internet access." I've seen the e-mails—I just haven't been able to get myself to respond.

"I do understand, Mr. Johnson," he says, beaming.

I catch Dodson rolling his eyes.

I'm not in Dodson's office for long. Mr. Ross gives me his business card and an MIT pen, and I leave after the late bell rings.

●

I walk into the Lion's Den, ignoring the stares that follow me, and stop at my usual lunch table with G-mo and Ivy.

"You missed it," G-mo says to me, putting down his hot dog drenched in ketchup and mayo. "There was just another fight that broke out. Some freshman beat up Lance Anderson. He got dragged out of here with a bloody nose. Yo, it was awesome!"

Ivy laughs. "That's what his ass get, too."

She pulls up a chair for me, and I sit down.

"Him getting kicked in the balls by a freshman was my favorite thing ever," G-mo says through a mouthful. "That's probably the highlight of this school year for everybody, yo. Shit, I would've done it myself."

"You don't have the balls," Ivy says, tossing grapes in her mouth.

"Yo, I have great balls. My balls hang like they don't have a curfew," G-mo answers.

Ivy play-punches him while laughing.

I shake my head and look around. I honestly would've

loved to see Lance Anderson get his racist ass kicked. I would love watching that video over and over again, rather than Tyler getting shot. Three times.

"You okay?" Ivy asks me. "You're pretty quiet. I mean, rightfully so, but—"

"I'm a'ight," I lie.

"You sure you a'ight?" Ivy presses. "I told you you don't need to lie to us." She opens up a bag of Sour Patch Kids and offers me some. I reach in and grab a few, making sure I don't take any yellow ones.

"Yeah, is there anything we can do?" G-mo adds.

I look up and they've got these concerned looks on their faces, and G-mo completely stops chewing. But before I can say anything, my phone vibrates. I pull it out of my pocket and see an e-mail. An e-mail from Albert Sharp. Instantly, my heart is beating fast and my hands are starting to shake.

I read the e-mail out loud, my eyes wide.

Dear Mr. Marvin Johnson,

Thank you for contacting me. I have been following this case, and I feel I must help you in this fight for justice. I have scheduled a community demonstration for December 25, 2018. I believe in the power of reminding

American citizens that black families are
grieving while others are celebrating. The
details are attached to this e-mail. May your
loved one rest in peace and power.

Albert Sharp
Director of the National Crisis Foundation

I gasp.

And a quick grin appears on my face, and then fades.

I open the attachment and see that we're going to have a
protest on the entire block by Sojo High, and it's on the same
day as Lance's protest in defense of the cop because he got
arrested for what he did. It's about a month away. After the
hearing.

"We gotta protest. We gotta protest for Tyler," I say. I'm
so glad Mr. Sharp is willing to help us I could cry.

Ivy lets out a breath and nods, twisting her Nautica hat
backward.

I squeeze my hands into my pockets and try to slow down
my heart, but it doesn't seem to work. I'm so mad that I feel
this weak.

· 21 ·

A Not-So-Happy Thanksgiving comes and goes—Mama and I having to fill the emptiness at the table with stories about Tyler, like how he'd eat all the dinner rolls up every year and about how he'd remind us how thankful he was for his family. Two weeks later, in early December, the preliminary hearing finally comes around. The grief comes in calmer waves now, though it still wreaks total havoc on my life. I'm numb and broken and it gets physically hard to breathe at times, but I still manage to get dressed in the morning. I put on an old suit and tie—the one and only suit and tie that I've ever owned, one that I got when my grand-father passed away. It's a bit too tight around the cuffs, and the legs are a lot thinner than I am. I squeeze into it and just stare at myself in the mirror.

"Ready?" Mama kisses me on the forehead, squeezing my arm.

"As ready as I can be," I say, my voice quivering.

●

Mama and I meet Faith and stand in line on the sidewalk outside the courthouse, a trail of people in front of us wait-ing for the doors to open. I asked Faith to come because she's been through this. She knows what to expect. Ivy's mom brings Ivy and G-mo up to the courthouse, and they take turns hugging me for the longest, and then we wait in silence for what feels like eternity even after the doors open, the line inching forward every few minutes.

The sky is a mixture of sapphire and sandstone, blazing down on us, and there's a slow, steady breeze. Once we're let in, an officer guides us down marble hallways and up a flight of stairs and into a cramped courtroom with white walls and seats made of old mahogany. The first thing I notice is that the room is mostly packed with people. Some spectators shuffle in and whisper, eyes fixed on Mama and me like we're the causes of every tragedy in the world. Others have looks of sympathy on their faces. And Mama just looks at the floor, fidgeting with a dirty Kleenex.

I see familiar faces that I recognize from school.

I see strange faces.

I see police officers, and this in particular is what gets me to start worrying.

The bailiff shows me and Mama to the front, where we've got designated seats behind the assistant district attorney, a white lady, who turns around to shake Mama's hand, and then it gets so painfully silent I can hear Mama's heart beating.

Mama nudges me in the side, a deep gasp slipping from her mouth. She points to a door. A line of police officers file in, strangely detached looks on their faces, like this is all too familiar for them, like they know that they've got nothing to worry about.

And then I see him. The officer. The one who took my brother away from me. I know his face from the news reports. From at night, when I close my eyes. A swelling rage washes over me, and I have to stop myself from getting to my feet, screaming shit at him, screaming that he took my brother away from me and Mama.

It's almost as if he makes an effort not to look our way. He was arrested shortly after the video leaked, but of course he immediately posted bail. He was given the kind of benefit of the doubt that they'd never give to Tyler. Or me. From his seat at the table across the aisle, the cop nods to the other officers.

I can't believe how they're treating him. This man killed my brother, and he got escorted in like he was the victim. This man killed my brother, and his family has the same number of seats in the courtroom as us. This man killed my brother, and we have to go through all this torture just to get justice. All I know is if Tyler were a white kid and the killer were black, things would be going a very different way. I just know it. They always do.

I draw in a deep breath and turn around and see Faith and Ivy and G-mo sitting, all looking a mix of the nerves and anger and sadness that I'm feeling.

The bailiff shouts, "All rise for the Honorable Judge Richard Watts!"

And everyone stands.

The room stills.

My heart feels like it's literally trying to beat, beat, beat its way out of me.

Mama reaches for my hand, and for a split second I consider pulling away. I don't want her to know how much I'm shaking right now. But then, as I grab her hand, I'm reminded that I'm not alone in this. That this feeling ripping me apart on the inside is something we share.

The bailiff continues, spewing words that don't quite make sense to me, and he stays still—so still, his voice so monotonous. "...the presence of the flag of our nation and the emblem of our Constitution in department forty-seven, we are now in session. Please be seated."

The judge clears his throat into the microphone in front of his face. He leans forward, his white, bald head reflecting the square, pale light above him. His glasses rest at the end of his nose as he scans the crowd.

I think to myself, *Here's the beginning of everything.*

· 22 ·

The room is a stark and startling white, except for the seats. I notice that a lot of people are wearing white, too, and it suddenly feels like I'm allergic to the world. My palms itch. My neck is sweating. My throat is scratchy, and everything blurs in my eyes, like I'm stuck in a pool of poison ivy, drowning in it.

The ADA is talking about the video now, explaining the last few minutes of Tyler's life. I squeeze my eyes shut so fucking tight when they play the video, but I can still hear my brother's voice. Hear the man who murdered him. But they don't call it that. No one is saying the *M* word.

And all I want to scream is: *Murder, man! It was fucking murder. Just because a goddamn crooked cop did it doesn't mean it's any less than that.*

The defense attorney speaks up. "Objection! Inconclusive. We've all reviewed it, and it's clear that he resisted."

The room starts blurring before me.

Tyler had a mother who loved him to bits—sometimes it felt like she loved him more than she loved me. Tyler had dreams—had the world at his fingertips and a whole life to live. Tyler had *me*.

But to them, all they see is his hoodie and baggy pants. All that cop saw was a thug looking for trouble.

He was just a kid.

Scratch that. I'm sick of the word *just* because Tyler wasn't *just* anything.

Tyler was my best friend, my companion all those times when I needed one. He was everything—everything—and just like that, he's not.

The world is muffled in my ears, and it sounds like I'm in a glass jar and there are vibrations bouncing off me, not quite clear, like I am floating in a hazy vertigo.

I'm not gonna cry, I keep reminding myself over and over, until I trick myself into believing it.

I force myself to block everything out as I replay one of my fondest memories with Tyler, a memory I hold on to tight, like the last hug we shared. It's a cloudy day, the earth soft, and the world smells like rain will fall soon. It's just the two of us on the court, and we're playing a game of one on one.

Tyler has the ball. He dribbles and dips and crosses me over as I try to play defense, my arms guarding him the best I can.

But he always finds ways to get around me. He dribbles the ball in between his legs, spins, releases the ball into the air, and then *SWOOSH!* The ball falls from the hoop and bounces a couple times on the ground before he checks it to me.

I dribble, breathing in, keeping my eyes on him, knowing his every move—mastering them.

We're both just sweat and nothing else, not saying anything, just playing.

●

A dark-skinned girl in a tight purple dress steps forward. When she walks to the stand in front of Mama and me, I can see her eyes up close. They aren't filled with tears, but with rage. She takes the oath, swearing on the Bible to tell the whole truth.

"State your name into the microphone, please," the judge says to her.

The girl runs a hand through her hair, flips it, and then says, "Daphne Haywood. I witnessed what happened the night of Tyler Johnson's slaughter, when he was stopped and then shot to death."

"Objection!"

"Sustained," the judge says. "We haven't come to a conclusion just yet, Ms. Haywood."

And I'm shaking so fucking bad right now. My life is not a movie, but most of the time I wish it were, and right now is one of those moments when I just fucking wish that this wasn't real. That the stories on the news, the stories from Mama, the stories Tupac rapped about had just been that. Stories. Not things that could happen to ordinary people. And I feel this harder, more than ever.

And I want to shout: *He was murdered. He was murdered.* But shouting this would be like shouting into a vacuum in space, only to be silenced and suffocated to death in the end.

The ADA begins questioning Daphne. "For the record, Ms. Haywood, are you a student at Sojourner Truth High School?"

"No, ma'am."

"How did you end up at the scene?"

"I was invited to the party by a friend's boyfriend."

"What did you do when the chaos started?"

"When I first heard gunshots, I dipped out, taking the back exit. When I got outside, that's when I saw Tyler. He didn't see me. The cop didn't see me either. At least, I don't think so, because neither of them took their eyes off each other."

"What did you see happen between Tyler and Officer Meredith?"

"The cop told Tyler to put his hands up in the air. Tyler dropped a package as he lifted up his arms. The cop had his gun pointed at Tyler the whole time, taking slow steps forward. I had a feeling that I knew what was going to happen. So I started recording with my phone."

"And then?"

"It was exactly like what is in the video. That's how I saw it. Tyler said that he just wanted to get home, and he pushed the cop away and started to run, and as soon as I heard three shots, I ran, but I made sure to keep recording." She stops and turns her head to look at Officer Thomas Meredith, her face angled up in disgust. "That boy didn't deserve that. Hell, no one does. And I'm sick and tired of these racist cops saying that he was just a thug and had it coming to justify their actions. This has happened in our community too damn much."

"Objection!" the defense attorney calls out, adjusting his black tie.

"Sustained."

"No further questions, Your Honor."

Now the defense attorney steps up to cross-examine her, his white face almost as red as his beard.

"Can you describe the party for the court?"

"The party was like all the others that I've been to, but it turned into everyone's worst nightmare. Gang fight and police raid all in one night."

"Noted. So, you were aware there was the potential for gang violence and police intervention?"

"Yes. But no one tells you when there's going to be a gang fight or a police raid."

"So, you're saying that you went to this party oblivious to the consequences?"

"What?"

"Objection, relevance!"

"Sustained."

"Withdrawn. When you exited the party, did you see Mr. Johnson handcuffed?"

"I don't think I saw handcuffs come out at all. Gun first. It was just the two of them going back and forth before the cop shot him."

"They were going back and forth? So, Mr. Johnson was resisting?" They're trying to get her like bait. And I want to scream.

"No. He was just asking why he was being targeted, which

anyone would do if they were scared. The officer didn't have to resort to the gun as his first option."

"Did he resist? Was he behaving violently toward Officer Meredith?"

The Tyler Johnson I knew, not the one the world is trying to make him out to be, was not violent. It doesn't matter if he wore his pants below his waist, had weed, or had all Ds and Fs on his sixth-grade report card—none of that gives a police officer the right to kill a kid.

And Daphne says it for me: "If in this country we want to justify murder for white people, for cops, I don't want to be here."

"Let's back up. Didn't you say it was dark?"

"Yes." She blinks real slow.

"How do you know what you saw, then?"

"It wasn't that dark. There was a streetlight. It's in the video. You can see for yourself, if you'd just open your damn eyes."

"If you're so sure that what you saw was murder, why did you stay, pull out your phone, and attempt to record what was going on instead of getting help?"

"I didn't stay." Daphne sighs before giving me a sad look. "When I heard the shots, I ran. I told no one about what I saw at first." And I can't exactly blame her for recording and not running to get help first. Because what help could she have gotten, if the people we go to for help are the very ones doing the harm? We're too familiar with shit like this. Tyler wasn't the first, and all the cases before him ended in the same way: no justice.

"You didn't tell anyone?"

"No," she says, taking a deep breath, her purple dress expanding at her stomach. "I panicked. I didn't know what to do. I didn't want to be next."

The entire room almost seems to freeze over. It gets so bitterly quiet.

"How did you know Mr. Tyler Johnson?"

"I didn't," she says. "Not until word got back to me from my friend's boyfriend about who it was in the video."

"Is that why you leaked the video anonymously?"

"I was scared," she replies. "And I didn't know what to do."

"So, apparently, you took it upon yourself to keep Mr. Tyler Johnson's death your little secret."

Each time they say his name, my heart beats faster.

"That's not what I said," Daphne goes. She flips her hair and sighs so angrily, so annoyed.

"No further questions, Your Honor."

As Daphne leaves the stand, she turns to Mama and me and mouths the words *I'm sorry* before going to find her seat.

I feel like I'm suffocating, taking my final gasp of air over and over again. I just want to scream for the world to listen closely, to listen carefully, to finally hear me. But I shake my head, unable to form any words. Everything in my mind is like a whirlpool, a free-for-all.

Mama starts sobbing into her Kleenex again. I spend the rest of the hearing focused on Mama or trapped in my own head, unable to concentrate on what the lawyers are discussing. Unable to trust that justice is coming our way.

· 23 ·

Mama and I practically have to be wheeled out of the room by bailiffs and security guards. And when their hands are on me, I flinch and cringe, a loud pang of disgust and anger inside. It takes a herculean effort for me to breathe, to remember that this is standard procedure, to remember that they mean me no harm.

As we exit the courthouse, there are reporters on the sidewalk asking Mama for a comment. She slides me behind her and starts talking into their microphones, telling the world about the boy she raised. How he was a good kid.

Never in trouble with the law. How he deserved better than to be shot and taken away from us. She tells everybody some of her fondest memories of Tyler as a child, some memories that I don't even remember myself.

"The entire city of Sterling Point is divided because of this man. Because of this broken system. Because of the hate Officer Meredith's brought onto us all. There are bad people in the world. That means there are bad cops. But there's also so much good. I just lost a son. My son just lost his brother. We've been living with the pain of his absence for what already feels like years. That man took something from me that I can never have back. All I'm asking is for some justice, and for help getting this officer off the street, because so many other kids are in danger. That's all."

I don't care what these reporters say or what the judge says or what anyone else thinks. I know that Tyler didn't deserve to die, no matter what. I'm going to do whatever I have to do to make sure that there's justice for Tyler.

●

The very moment we pull into the driveway, rain starts falling from clouds in the sky—the clouds that kind of resemble the hurt in my heart—and when we get out, Mama stumbles into the house.

I stand in the rain. Mama believes that when it rains,

family members who have crossed over to the other side use the drops to tell us things, and I'm left thinking maybe Tyler's in heaven, whispering things to the drops of rain as they trip on their tiny tails and splatter onto the earth, and I imagine that they know how it is to be black in America, to have a destiny of falling, to have a fate of dying on impact.

It's in this moment that I'm reminded of something Auntie Nicola told me—that life's not about waiting for the storm to pass, because sometimes it never does—and all of a sudden, I feel waves of emotion engulfing me. Life is about *wading* in the rain, in all the storm's fury, holding on to hope, and also becoming one and the same with the storm—getting angry, getting heated, and being the change you want.

●

I change into a pair of joggers and a T-shirt, and then I text G-mo and Ivy, inviting them over, and within minutes, like the world's best friends, they come climbing through my window like they used to, all wet and alert, unsettled looks on their faces.

"'Sup, Marv?" Ivy says, climbing through first, clenching her skateboard under her arm.

"Yo, hey, Marv." G-mo pats my shoulder. "Everything all right?"

And I just plop down on the edge of my bed, not answering, looking at his Slytherin tank top.

And then Ivy diverts things, saying, "Can you believe someone just tried to steal my skateboard and G's bike? In the pouring goddamn rain. Like, what the fuck, bro?!"

I look up, feeling hollowed out, and I mumble, slightly shaken, "What happened?"

"We scared 'em away," G-mo answers. "Straight up, yo, fists up ready to bump and everything."

Ivy rolls her eyes, a smirk easing onto her face. "Something like that. More like we just pedaled and skated faster down the block." She pauses and then walks over and sits down beside me.

"Whoa" is all that comes out. I sigh.

"How're you feeling, Marv?" Ivy asks.

"I have this horrible, horrible feeling in my gut, like I'm trapped in some goddamn fucked-up movie," I say, brushing my clammy hands against my pants. "My brother's a fucking hashtag. Everybody thinks he was a thug."

I want to fuck something up. Punch someone. Blow up something.

G-mo sits next to me now and wraps his arm around the back of my neck, like old times. "Yo. I'm down to go fuck some shit up," G-mo says. "I fucking hate white people, and man, fuck the police!"

"Nigga, that's racist!"

"You can't be racist if you're a minority," G-mo argues. "Prejudiced? Yes. But not racist. We ain't got the power in this society to be racist. And they want war!"

"Fool, the war started a long time ago," Ivy says. "It ain't even black against white, bro," she continues calmly, using her hands to punctuate her words. "It's about racists against everyone else, and they're clownin' out."

G-mo sighs and falls back on the bed.

"It's like Tupac said: Everybody's at war," Ivy adds as she jumps up and stands straight. "Why you think he had a whole album about that shit?"

"Yo. You right, you right," G-mo goes.

Mama's in the kitchen, pots and pans rattling together in a cacophonous symphony. I sit still, thinking Ivy's right. It's about the hate some people have within them. Hate is too ugly of a devil for some people to acknowledge, but the thing about hate is you can't throw it on someone else without getting a little bit on yourself. And I wonder if people will ever fucking understand that.

· **24** ·

The next morning, the news channels continue their reports on Tyler.

The camera zooms in on a news reporter's pale face. "The victim's father, Jamal Johnson, is in Montgomery Correctional Facility for possession of illegal narcotics and capital murder."

My fists ball up. There's something about being reminded of this—the truth—in such a painful way that just kills what little feeling I have left in me. For so long, I felt that the way out of my own suffering was to pretend it didn't exist—to put a blindfold on to the whole white world thing that Mama kept warning me about. But this has done so much damage— damage that I can't even really see. Maybe we don't see until it's too late, but I'm seeing that just because the world shits on you doesn't mean you fucking deserve it.

The reporter begins interviewing an older black dude with gray hair and a poufy mustache. I recognize him immediately from all the research, from looking at his website over and over again, watching for updates on the protest he's planning for Tyler. His name flashes across the screen. Albert Sharp.

"What do you think of the case?" the reporter woman asks.

Mr. Sharp scratches his eyebrow before answering. "It's truly saddening what our country is facing," he says, his voice moving like molasses.

"Care to explain?" the news reporter says into a microphone.

"Well, you know, for many years, our country has faced severe racial tension, discrimination, prejudice, and violence on all levels. We've heard of many cases like this one with Tyler Johnson, where unarmed black teenagers are brutalized by the police. We need to stand up as a community, as a nation, as a people, and combat this issue."

"So, what do you think will happen now?" the reporter asks.

"Communities, I hope, will gather and show their respect first and foremost, but I believe there is definitely a divide in our area. And I also strongly believe that it's up to everyone, regardless of race, to heal that divide and come together to fight police brutality."

"Thank you for your time."

I sit close to Mama on our small slashed-up couch, feeling numb all over. And it's in this moment that I start to feel sorry for myself again, and I'm not sure if that's at all what I'm supposed to be feeling, but it's consuming.

· 25 ·

When I go back to school two days after the hearing, news of Lance Anderson's protest has spread to just about every Sojo High teacher, every student, every janitor, and this means that everyone's now having serious, hard, racially charged discussions for once in the school's history. Sojo High, though predominantly black and Hispanic, is still divided. Even schools in the hood have their share of racists.

This is too much. This is killing me.

I need to get to a safe place where I don't have to be eyed

up and down, a place where I don't have to tell people that Tyler didn't just die—that he was killed. A place where I don't have to say the obvious—a place where people don't hate other human beings for the color of their skin.

Suddenly, I'm wondering what's going to happen at our protest for Tyler. Are people going to try to stop it from happening? Will crooked police gather and try to silence those of us who are asking for a change? It's happened before. Why wouldn't it happen again?

The rest of the school day is a chaotic blur of people whispering their hate and offering their condolences. And I realize I've come back too soon. I'm not ready to be around so many people acting like they knew who my brother really was. I need more time.

●

After school, G-mo, Ivy, Faith, and I meet up at G-mo's place, and we start getting ready for the protest. It's going to be on the street in front of Sojo High.

"The streets are gonna be flooded with racists, yo!" G-mo rasps.

"Yeah, so many," Ivy says. "I already know."

They're right—and that's why we have to outnumber them.

We've got the news on G-mo's small, twelve-inch TV,

and they're talking about the hearing and asking people to answer their online poll on whether or not the officer is guilty.

He's guilty. There shouldn't be any question or a stupid damn online poll about it.

Faith's whole face looks how I feel, and she watches me with these huge, warm, brown eyes. Then she stands and hugs me, her hand on the back of my head.

"I want to help," she says, and I think that's really all I wanted to hear from her, from anyone. "Tell me what I can do to help."

"Join us," I tell her, pulling back. "Invite everyone you know."

Faith nods. "My mother's friend is a cop. He's a good guy named Paulie. He's outraged by what happened. I'll see what he can do for us, too."

"Perfect."

We spend all night inviting people and making signs and posting things on Twitter and Facebook and Tumblr.

We even get one new hashtag trending.

#TylerJohnsonWasHere

· 26 ·

When I wake up on Christmas Day—the day of the protest—there's a really bad taste in my mouth. My eyes flicker open around 3:00 AM, and I think maybe someone's going to climb through my window in the middle of the night and off me, and instead of getting up I just remain in bed, thinking about what'll happen today. Either something or nothing at all.

In the kitchen, Mama has tea made and she's on the phone with Auntie Nicola, and they're talking about the protest happening today. I watch her squeeze lemon into a mug.

"Morning. Merry Christmas," she says after she tells Auntie Nicola she'll call back later. Nothing feels *merry*. Mama kisses my forehead and wipes the sleep from my eyes. "Feeling okay?" She gives me such a bittersweet look.

"Just got this gut feeling that something bad is going to happen. I got this gut feeling that this'll never end."

She reaches for my hand and squeezes.

"I made some tea over there," she says with a hole in her voice as she points to the kitchen table, Tyler's pictures still scattered across it. It's become her morning routine to look at them and grieve and cry and pray to God to deliver the world from hate.

"Thanks." I breathe out. "Anything that'll help."

I pour some tea into a little glass and take a sip. Mama puts the back of her hand to my forehead before she moves it to my cheek. "Making sure you don't have a stress cold," she says. "I think I'm coming down with one."

"I'll be fine."

"Nervous 'bout the protest?" she asks. "I can see so much worry in your eyes, boy." Her voice cracks, and I wish I could wedge myself inside it.

"Kind of," I reply after a pause. "I think it's important that I'm there."

She shakes her head. Once upon a time, Mama would've exploded, saying, *No—you're not going to that. These streets ain't never been safe, and they most certainly ain't safe for you now. I done lost one; I ain't losing two.* But now—now, she just gives me a small, warm smile and opens her arms.

We hug and she kisses my hairline and I'm nodding and tearing up against her chest.

"We can't *not* get involved with this," I say.

"I know, baby," she responds.

"If we stay quiet, if we don't fight back, if we let them silence us, we're sending them a signal that they can keep doing this mess."

She clears her throat and blinks. Her gaze then falls to the floor, and I can see the gears in her mind starting to turn as she remains quiet.

Feeling a chill strike up my spine, I add, "We can't give them this, Ma."

She exhales. "I'm proud of you." She grabs the teapot from the table, pours some more in her little white mug, and picks up one of the photos of Tyler, gazing at it with regret in her blinking eyes.

●

Mama and I move to the living room and flip on the news. People are already starting to gather for the protest. I see a blend of people, and signs, and all sorts of flags. It's all so overwhelming, and I can't really think straight.

On the news, there're clips of police squad cars with their blinking headlights and military tanks rolling past protestors on both sides of the road, and the anchorman talks about how this is all supposed to be a "peaceful protest."

There've been so many protests throughout history, and a lot of them didn't end peacefully. I don't know if this one will. Seeing all these cops with their weapons has me nervous. Yes, I'm willing to die for this cause, but the fact that there's even a chance that I'll die, become a hashtag, be remembered briefly, and then be completely forgotten and marked as a statistic fucking terrifies me.

The news anchorman, who has the whitest button-up to match his skin, hair long gone, is describing the protestors— the ones who are advocates for justice, the ones who want the best for the world, the ones who want to do the right thing. His words cause an uneasy pang in my stomach. *Violent tendencies. Angry. Thugs.*

The screen flashes a glimpse of angry white folks screaming so loud the veins in their necks show, and they are screaming messed-up stuff, like *"RID OUR STREETS OF THE THUGS!"* And everybody knows that that's a fucked-up code for KILL THE BLACKS.

"When will they see that it's not okay to kill us?" I can feel the shaking in my hands.

Mama purses her lips. "Honey, I wish I knew. The racism

in their hearts is like seeds that sprout roots. Racism can always be uprooted, though." She places a hand on her chest, like she's feeling her heart giving out—or in, a little too much.

I put a fist up to my open mouth. "I have to go."

As I turn to head to my room to get changed, she grabs my elbow and pulls me back. "You need to come back alive. No fighting. No talking back to the police. Keep your hands up high in the air. Go with nothing in your pockets. Keep your mouth shut, and the likelihood of surviving is solid enough," she says, tears flooding her eyes.

Her words are fucking tough and make me uncomfortable as shit. But they're necessary and important. And I'm hoping G-mo's, Ivy's, and Faith's mothers told them the same thing mine just told me.

The smell of the honey in the tea turns my stomach some more. Or maybe it's what Mama said, but I think she's definitely right. The best way to ensure your survival at a protest is to act like you're invisible, even when you're not.

She releases me and folds her arms.

Back in my room, I flip through the messages and tags on my phone. One message from Ivy says: Where u at? Another text from Faith says: Let me know when u are ready. I'll pick u up.

I dig into my closet to find something to wear. I scroll

through a few hangers of plaid shirts and polos, and Mama knocks on my door, creaking it open to peek her head through.

"I'm going with you," she says, wiping her eyes. "I'm not letting you go alone."

We exchange nods and sad smiles. She's changed into black boots, a black T-shirt, and black jeans, and she put a pair of black sunglasses on top of her head, as if she's the newest Black Panther.

I put on black, too. A black hoodie. Some black shoes. And the darkest jeans I can find in my dresser drawers. The hoodie and jeans are both a couple sizes bigger than I usually like, but they make me feel powerful, in control, and whole.

I text Faith that I'll meet her at the protest, and that Mama is going to take me.

●

It's all so damn shocking to me as we pull up to the protest. We can't even park or get close enough to the front of Sojo High because there're so many people walking and standing, even sitting, in the street.

So Mama parks all the way around the corner, and we weave our way through the crowd until I find Ivy and G-mo. The two of them greet me with huge hugs.

"Shit's been going down," G-mo says, putting a hand on my shoulder, and then he hugs Mama.

"For real, though. They brought out the dogs on one dude because he crossed the boundary," Ivy says, pointing ahead of us at an orange line drawn on the ground with spray paint or something. "And they was about to throw tear gas."

I look around, seeing so many strangers, Sojo High students, police officers, other people draped in Confederate *and* American flags on the other side of the line. Lots of people holding up signs. And I'm scanning everywhere, wondering if all hell is about to break loose, trying to convince myself that this isn't a fucked-up scene from some dystopian movie.

There're huge police lines, vans, and cones on every corner, containing us in a single space. Like animals or criminals. At the ends of each road are SWAT trucks and huge military tanks, as if they're a symbol to prevent us from escaping oppression.

There are newsmen and newswomen here in fancy suits, with microphones glued to their hands and pressed up against the mouths of Sojo High students. Half of Sojo High is out joining this fight, this desperate plea for justice and safety—basic human rights.

"Everyone stay close by," I say, leading the way deeper into the crowd to the front line of the protest. I start to see people I recognize, even some from Johntae's party.

"Aye-yo! There goes Faith!" G-mo shouts, pointing her out as she comes from an alley across the way.

Faith runs over and throws her arms around me, her braids scratching the side of my face. She passes us bullhorns and large white signs.

As we move to the front of the protest, I see the posters up close. Some have my brother's name on them, and also a list of other names. Some of them say: TYLER'S FREE! Because, I realize, it's all about how he's free. It's not just about how he died. It's about how he broke free in such a fucked-up way. It's about how he lived.

Ivy's sign, held up high in the sky, says: STAY WOKE.

G-mo's sign says: I AM A HUMAN BEING. I AM YOU.

The sign that I hold up says in big, bold, black letters: MY LIFE MATTERS!

There's a cacophonous blare of voices that has me flinching.

Everything is so loud and suffocating.

I turn my head and see Ms. Tanner waving us down. When she finally gets over to us, she hugs everyone, even my mom.

I give yet another scan of the crowd to see all types of people: black, white, Asian, Latino, young, and old. And I see Albert Sharp. He stands surrounded by news reporters, by protestors, but when he sees Mama and me, he steps right toward us and first takes Mama's hands, then my own. His palms are warm and dry. Everyone nearby turns to look at us, and I can feel realization sweeping over the crowd—realization of who we are, that we're Tyler Johnson's family.

"I'm glad you came," Mr. Sharp says, his voice just as deep and slow as molasses as it was on the news. "I know this is a difficult time for you. But we will get justice. For you, and for your son," he says to Mama.

She's nodding slowly, eyes tearing up. "Thank you."

He nods at me with a small smile. "You've got a great young man here," he says. "Contacted me about getting this protest set up."

Mama looks at me with surprise, but I shrug, embarrassed. "I felt like I couldn't just sit there. I had to do something."

He puts a hand on my shoulder. "I'm sorry for the pain you're feeling."

Mr. Sharp tells us that God's going to come through in the end, that he always does, that he's going to push us right out of this messy tunnel in our lives. He even stops to pray for us, asking the Lord for mercy and grace and peace and justice. Everyone around circles us, including Ivy and G-mo and Faith, their hands reaching in to touch us while we pray—and whether they believe in God or not, whether they're praying with us or not, I know they're reaching in so that we'll know we're not alone. We'll know there're people who want justice for Tyler, too. That they're hurting also. It's enough to make the pain bubble up, and tears leak from my eyes. Faith keeps her hand on my shoulder the whole time.

When Albert Sharp finishes his prayer, we stand in a straight line, holding hands, megaphones in front of our faces. And we start chanting. Our chant is simple, and it doesn't take long for everyone to join in, to become one powerful roar of voices, wanting and needing so desperately to be heard.

"Sterling Point P-D, stop brutality! Sterling Point P-D, stop brutality!" We chant this on a loop, getting louder each time, until our voices crack and dry. And we all do a rally wave—like effect, where one person starts to raise their hands in the air and shout, "Don't shoot me!" and then everyone else follows.

As the sun beams and blinds me, I put a hand over my eyes like a visor and look across the way, but I can't quite hide from the hate. There's a line of angry police officers wearing bulletproof vests and helmets, with plastic shields in one hand and rifles in the other. Some cops are holding leashes attached to equally pissed Rottweilers with foamy mouths and spiky collars. They got all this military gear. For a while, I just take in everything I see, listening to Mama and Ivy and G-mo and Faith shout the chants beside me.

I hear another kind of screaming. I look back over at the line of police officers, and I see a few of them on top of a protestor, one of them with his knee in the protestor's back as he lies sprawled on the ground. A black kid who just keeps repeating that his phone isn't a gun, but they don't even give a shit. They slap on the cuffs anyway.

A phone isn't dangerous, I tell myself, *and neither is black skin.*

Ivy clears her throat. "Listen up, ladies and gentlemen," she shouts into the megaphone. All the chaos and noise comes down to a whisper. "We are here today for a few different reasons! To fight for our homie Tyler Johnson. To take a stand against police brutality and demand change and justice for all. We're here to say we've had enough. No more. We shouldn't be afraid of the people who're supposed to protect us. We just shouldn't have to be. Peace and equality shouldn't be this hard."

The crowd cheers and applauds, and I feel Faith's arm loop with mine as she rests her head on my shoulder, her hand on my chest as if she needs to feel my heartbeat, to know that I am not going to combust from all the feelings pent up inside me.

Ivy slips out her phone and reads something off the screen. "Our lives matter! Oscar Grant mattered! Freddie Gray mattered! Michael Brown mattered! Jordan Davis mattered! Eric Garner mattered! Tarika Wilson mattered! Dontre Hamilton mattered! Sandra Bland mattered! Trayvon Martin mattered! Tanisha Anderson mattered! Yvette Smith mattered! Tamir Rice mattered! Alton Sterling mattered! Philando Castile mattered! Jordan Edwards mattered! Don't forget—Emmett Till mattered!"

The last one sticks and makes me feel nauseous: *"Tyler Johnson mattered!"* I raise my fist, all clenched and tight. Ivy, G-mo, Faith, Mama, and a bunch of others put their fists in the air, too. And we look like an ocean of multicolored fists. The fist in the air originated as a symbol of black power and pride, but it's also a symbol of solidarity and unity, and I think the fact that so many protestors showed up says a lot about how we stand as a people, and about how we can bring change. Together.

I look to my left when I see something move out the corner of my eye. I notice a kid wearing a white T-shirt with #TYLERJOHNSONWASHERE written in thick black Sharpie breaking away from the crowd and walking closer and closer to the cops. The dogs are barking, and the boy—a white boy I recognize from Ms. Tanner's class—stomps his feet hard on the ground to send the dogs jumping back. It only makes them more pissed.

I think to myself, *I don't know what he's about to do, but it's not going to be good.*

It feels like the world is moving slower as the boy crosses over the cutoff line, entering into dangerous territory.

Suddenly, the line of police officers breaks and disperses into our crowd. I hear a few bangs and pops. Rubber bullets hail down on my skin like sharp droplets from the sky.

Bodies fall over, crying out.

Rage and hate in the eyes of the people who're supposed to be protecting us.

People run in all directions, and I lose Faith, Ivy, G-mo, and Mama in the crowd. I spin around, looking for Mama, trying to find her in the mess of faces blurring by, cringing in pain. I run down the block, away from the chaos, and stand there, looking at it all with my hands on my head.

My lungs feel tight.

Feet heavy.

I hear the shattering of glass. I turn to my left and see a group of people with ski masks on and bats in hand busting the windows out of nearby cars and school buses and news vans.

No, I say to myself. *This isn't how this is supposed to go.*

Faith comes running toward me. She links arms with me.

"What do you wanna do?" she says. "Join the riot? If these pigs want to play dirty, we can, too. Two can play that game."

What the hell, Faith? No. I try to remind myself that I don't believe in violence. But a part of me wants to say fuck everything, fuck everybody, fuck the peace. If they want to do this, then we can get ugly back. And sometimes, anger is the only way to really get people to pay attention—to listen.

But I know this isn't how I want to remember Tyler. The rage built up in me isn't going to bring him back. I shake my head at Faith, and she nods, like she respects my decision. And we stand there and watch as the protest falls apart around us.

Some guys hop on top of cars and news vans, vandalizing and stomping on them. The shattering of glass plays on loop until there's no more unbroken glass in sight. The protestors don't leave Sojo Truth High intact either. The entrance door has dents in it, and its glass window is shattered. Some of the classroom windows have been beaten in as well.

I watch someone light a trash can on fire and throw it across the way toward the police cars, and suddenly it bursts into flames, creating a line of fire. Someone even tries setting a parked school bus on fire as a small crowd of people cheers, but they can't get it to work right. Instead, they just kick it, throw rocks at the windows, and destroy the seats on the inside.

I see a flash of Mama's face and run into the crowd to grab her arm. She's with Ivy and G-mo. I see dark purple lumps on her arm. She's been shot with rubber bullets.

I pull her over to the side where Faith is standing.

I collapse on the ground beside her. "Ma, Ma, Ma. You okay?" My heart is beating so fast inside my chest right now.

She nods and flinches when I try pulling her up, holding her arm.

"You sure?"

She lifts herself off the ground, moving her arm around. "I'm good." I brush her back and shoulders to remove all the dirt and rubble. She tries to get back out to the protest with everyone else.

I grab her arm again. "Where're you going? We should head home before this gets worse."

"Hell no," she snaps. "Tyler got a shot to the chest and two in the stomach and died. I'm gonna stay here and make my voice heard."

And that's exactly what she does.

The entire street becomes a panorama of oranges and reds and yellows. Fire everywhere. Rocks and bottles and cans fly through the air, and I can't keep up. We all try to stick together in a small group to protect one another from harm, but we're also shouting, "No justice, no peace!" and "We're so tired of this shit, man!" The muscles in my neck are starting to get sore from screaming. I can't believe we even have to do this.

People are suddenly wearing gas masks now. Others are using their shirts to cover their noses and mouths. I look behind me, and police are rushing toward us with firework cannons.

Boom! They fire into the crowd.

Boom! They fire again.

Smoke funnels everywhere on impact. I choke, and my eyes burn and water. And this anger inside my chest wants to come out. It's choking me and I can't breathe between these tears.

Fire trucks arrive, and the cops start spraying people with water. The ground becomes slick, and people slip and slide in the street.

Protestors are getting in their cars and moving to different areas, escaping the riot before the police start shooting real bullets.

Mama grabs me and we run to the car. Ivy, G-mo, and Faith follow behind. We all wheeze and wheeze for oxygen until we get away from the scene and can breathe in clean air.

Before, when I heard about black and brown kids getting killed by the police, I didn't think protesting was worth it, that it would do anything at all. I used to think that protests were stupid because they wouldn't change anything, especially not a racist's mind. But now I see: This is only the beginning of a long fight. It's my turn to speak up and resist.

· **27** ·

I can't draw worth shit, but I spend the next couple weeks sketching the same picture of a boy with a low fade and a wide nose, flat like a pug's, standing in front of a black hole, one leg engulfed in dark matter, the other in the light. It's been yet another failed experiment to distract myself, to worry less about whether Officer Monster will get indicted and put in jail for what he did.

I've tried everything, even drowning myself in my music, but nothing seems to work—nothing seems to stop the grief from grabbing me by the throat and choking the oxygen right out. I almost think that I get worse as each day passes. I sleep. I wake. I sleep. I wake. And I keep on doing that until they seem to become one and the same.

All my days are a hazy, unhappy mess inside my fragmented home, and outside my window, where real life waits in all of its shadows, the sun getting consumed by the hand of the night, I see white people walking happily down the street and it's a goddamn aching punch in the gut of something people like me don't quite yet have: freedom.

I wake up and eat my Lucky Charms slowly. I wake up wondering how many mornings and nights I've got left. I wake up trying to convince myself that it was all just a dream. But this only brings more grief. Because this shit isn't a dream, man.

One day my brother was here, and then the next, he wasn't.

And it's such a strange and depressing thing to wonder how many days it'll take for Mama to stop kissing Tyler's urn. How long it'll take for her to stop talking to it in the morning and at night.

My Mondays become Wednesdays and my Wednesdays become Fridays and my Fridays become Mondays again. At least, that's the way it seems. Time has become such an agonizing thing to bear. There's only this moment right now, the next one, and the one after that. And I realize that the saying was bullshit all along. Time does not heal. It only anesthetizes.

Mondays, Fridays, and Saturdays are days that I spend with Faith. And it's so nice to have her around. Her presence, though it comes in tiny doses, is like a drink that I down to blur out all the bad things that have happened in my life.

Faith's also teaching me how to be the *only* child, which guts me as much as it dulls all this hurt. But I find ways to turn the hurt into anger and the anger into lonely and the lonely into busy, even if it means trying to push through the pointless schoolwork Ms. Tanner drops off at my house every day and drawing shitty-ass stick figures and black blotches of ink.

Faith is doing work for her college one Monday night, flipping through a textbook. I sit on the edge of her bed, watching her, trying not to think about the fact that I have to get my application done since I got an extension, and I don't think I'll be able to. Isn't it fucked up that my brother is gone, and I might get to go to MIT because I fit the kind of black boy category they're looking for?

"What're you thinking about?" Faith asks, glancing up from her book.

"Nothing," I lie. She waits, and I let out a sigh. "Just about college. What I'm going to do."

"You're still being considered for MIT, right?"

I shrug. "Yeah."

"You seem so excited about that," she says with a small smile.

And the thing is, once upon a time, I really did think I was excited about it. "I used to be. Not so much anymore."

She closes her textbook. "Why not?"

"Because of everything. Tyler. I don't know."

"It can be hard to feel like you're moving on with your life. After Kayla died, I felt like I didn't have the right to go to school or anything like that."

I'm nodding, my eyes tearing up. I'm so fucking sick of crying.

She puts a hand on my knee. "You don't have to feel guilty."

"You know, before he died, I told him that he didn't have to do what was expected of him. Everyone looks at us and expects us to be into the drug life because we're black, and I told him he didn't have to go down that path. But I'm doing the same thing, in a way. Applying to MIT just because people say that's the best school to go to."

She opens her textbook again. "Sounds to me like you're not actually that excited about MIT."

●

When I get home, I tear open an Oatmeal Creme Pie and stare at my computer screen, looking at MIT's website.

And I exit out. Open up another tab and start looking at other colleges. Best schools to double-major in science and African-American history. Historically Black Colleges and Universities, like Howard University, where a lot of famous black people went. Taraji P. Henson, Chadwick Boseman, Diddy, Zora Neale Hurston, and even Thurgood Marshall.

My bedroom door creaks open.

"Hey." Mama smiles warmly at me. She's wearing a black-and-white sundress. "You've got a visitor."

I feel my eyebrows furrow. "Who is it?"

She places a hand on her hip.

I minimize my tabs and lift myself up to go check, walking down the hall and into the kitchen. A girl is sitting at the table, but she stands as soon as I walk in, chair scraping back against the tile. It's the girl from the hearing, Daphne, with a sweet potato pie in her hands.

She has a look in her eyes like she's hugging me in her head.

"What're you doing here?" I say, and immediately regret how rude I sound—but I don't like reminders of Tyler, don't like reminders of the hearing. And a part of me is pissed at Daphne, too—for being there, for being the last person to see Tyler alive besides his murderer, for just filming and not doing anything to stop it.

But I know it wasn't her fault. If she'd tried to stop the

officer, she might've gotten killed, too, and no one would've ever seen the video. Mama and I might still not have any idea what happened to Tyler.

She clears her throat, looking a little nervous. "I just want to say…I'm sorry," she says. "I would've stopped by sooner, but I didn't want to barge in while you're grieving." There's a pause and then she adds, "I wish I could say I don't know how you feel."

I still can't say anything back. I look down at the floor.

"I lost my cousin to police violence," she says. Mama stands at the kitchen doorway, staying quiet—so quiet, hands folded in front of her.

I just stand here like a deer in headlights, counting the length of my breaths. In my head, I tell her *I'm sorry*, but I can't say any words out loud. And it's like she understands.

Daphne starts walking closer to me, her arms falling to her sides. "Her name was Jasmine. She was only sixteen." She pauses and her fists clench. "We grew up together, y'know? And our mamas was just as close as us. Always smoking and gossiping together. Like all the other black kids in our hood, we grew up hearing the horror stories, but it always seemed like just a nightmare—not something real. But when we lost Jaz, that was when it finally hit me that it's all real."

I nod at her, swallowing the lump in my throat.

She keeps talking. "My pops used to warn us about the

police. He used to say, like all things in the world, there are good ones and bad ones. He used to say get a good look at the cop's face 'cause that makes all the difference. He used to say memorize the badge number or the license plate number. That's why I recorded what I saw after the party. Video footage seems like the only way people will even hear us sometimes."

I nod once again, almost whispering, *Yeah*. The only thing I can bring myself to say back is "How did you find me?"

And she replies, "You're famous. Not the good kind of famous, of course, but it wasn't that hard to find you."

Mama invites Daphne to stay awhile and then makes us dinner—and I mean a real dinner. Ever since Tyler died, there've been donations coming in from all over. Enough money, Mama says, to even send me to school. It won't bring him back, but it helps. We have fried catfish with hot sauce and macaroni and cheese. But the whole time, Mama and I keep exchanging looks as if we're reading each other's thoughts, because the seat where Tyler often sat is filled for at least a little while. And I'm not so sure whether that little while comforts Mama or breaks her on the inside.

Just last week, we had a vigil for Tyler. Faith, Ivy, and G-mo helped set everything up. It was in the park, and it had just stopped raining for the first time in three days, and it looked like the sky had literally fallen onto the earth. Everything was pitch-black, but scattered in random places were little lights—candles. On one of the benches, we had flowers and pictures of Tyler. It looked like the whole community showed up—strangers with Black Lives Matter posters, strangers with the thoughts of buried relatives weighing heavily on their shoulders. Strangers holding signs with names of black victims on them, and Tyler's in big fat letters. There were people from Sojo High there, too.

Auntie Nicola even called me up because she knew I was taking everything particularly hard, and reminded me that vigils are sort of like funerals, but they're to celebrate life, not death.

That whole night, until the sun slipped out from some hidden crack, we all prayed. We prayed for grace, we prayed for mercy, we prayed for change, we prayed for guidance, we prayed for one another, we prayed for protection, and we prayed for justice.

●

Every damn day for what feels like forever, I check the mail, hoping to find something about the judge's decision from the hearing. And then one day, there's a letter waiting with Mama's name on it in the mailbox. The yellow envelope has big red print and was sent from the hearing's judge and the state. The letter shocks the shit out of me, and I call Mama over. She tears it open, hands trembling, and I know her heart's probably beating just as hard as mine. We read the letter together, and the judge writes that they're going to take the case further so that there'll be a trial.

Mama puts the letter on the fridge, a Bo-Bo's gas station magnet holding it in place. And we keep carrying on as best we can with fake smiles. Maybe they're not even smiles. Imagine being sucker punched in the face every morning and smiling about it. I guess it's not a smile at all. It's just that you force all the muscles in your face to create the illusion of happiness.

· 28 ·

Today, I'm helping Faith study for her college exams. After we run through all the major historic events in the United States, attempting some geography of the world and geography of each other, we turn to economics. An hour or so after we finish studying, I read her the poem "Mother to Son" by Langston Hughes, my favorite poet of all time.

And life for me ain't been no crystal stair.

Faith exhales. "You know," she goes, leaning back against the headboard on her bed, "with as much reading as you do, you should try writing your own poem. Maybe even a book."

I attempt a laugh. And I just study her for a second, trying to figure out if she's making fun of me or not.

"I'm serious," she says. "I bet you could write a book about your life that'd sell a million damn copies."

I slide my pencil in the space behind my ear, and it stays in place. I inch a bit closer to her and say very softly, "I never thought about it, but maybe you're right. Maybe I should." My smile feels like it gets bigger. "And you'll be in the dedication."

"Nah," she says, "that'll just drive me wild."

"Why?"

"It just will," she says. I watch her glimmer.

"Yeah," I say. I am beginning to notice that my *ye-ah*s are almost like two separate syllables, like I've invented my own dialect to detach myself from the world. One syllable for *yes* and the other for *but everything may fall through in the end*.

She nods at me, her head to the side, just gazing and cheesing her cheesy smile.

"What do you want to be in the future?" I ask.

She flickers her eyes. "I want to be a designer." Her eyes move to scan her room, and I follow them, looking at the cutouts from magazines and newspapers plastered on her walls—things that she has stitched, glued, and taped together into her own creations.

And as she tells the stories behind all of the designs, it hits me: This is how she escapes. She runs away to *Teen Vogue* and *Ebony* magazines to disappear into the outside world, far, far away from Sterling Point. Making cutouts.

Right as she starts to explain one of the creations—a man wearing a tinfoil dress, a pair of white Jordans, and an alligator-skin hat—a scratchy voice calls out from one of the other rooms.

"Faith! Girl. Faiiiiith! Come here!"

"It's my mom," she says. "She's home early." Her shoulders slump and she rises from the bed, a surprised look on her face.

I sink into the bed.

"I'll be right back," she says, and winks.

"All right." I nod, stretching out and admiring the glow-in-the-dark stars on her ceiling. I keep quiet and listen to the back and forth between her and her mother.

When she gets back, she has laundry in her hands. She walks across her room and puts it on her bright pink beanbag chair. "I forgot to take my laundry out of the dryer," she sighs, brushing her hair back with her shoulder. "She gets super mad about that. It's old age. I swear." We share a quick laugh. She comes back over to the bed.

I turn my head slowly, and our lips lock. On impact, we

ignite. One thought in mind: *This feels a thousand times better than any word either of us could say.* And I'm trying my best to kiss her good enough that she forgets where she is, good enough that I forget everything, good enough that I fill with hope.

But I pull back. She puts a hand on mine.

"I know," she says quietly. "You don't have to feel guilty. It's okay to live. If you don't—then that cop took both your lives."

I nod, and she kisses me again, and the two of us lie down in her bed, side by side, and slowly tell each other embarrassing stories and then name the plastic stars on her ceiling.

"That one's Adelina," she says. "No, Artisha."

"There's Marcus," I say, pointing to a tiny one in the corner.

She laughs. "It looks more like a Devin." There's a pause and we're paying attention to each other's eyes. Then she breaks our gaze, pointing over our heads. "See those two together right there?"

"Mm-hmm," I answer.

"They're twins, and I'm naming them Marvin and Tyler." She smiles, still looking at the plastic stars on her ceiling.

Faith's mom, Ms. Gladys, walks in, offering some homemade trail mix. We both take handfuls, and Ms. Gladys does a double take with her eyes before walking out. "No shutting doors if you don't pay bills, Faith. You know that," she says.

Faith rolls her eyes and looks back at me with a grin.

"And leave some room for Jesus between y'all."

Faith and I chill for a little while longer, feeding each other trail mix, and then she drops me off at my place, the sun still on the verge of setting, like it's confused and indecisive.

· **29** ·

Did she let you do it without a condom?" is the first thing
G-mo says as he climbs through my window with Ivy.
For all the years we've been friends, I still don't know why
they don't just use the door, but I don't mind it. G-mo has
this huge, sneaky grin on his face, like I am full of dirty little
details and he's about to get an earful.

But all I say is "Shush, keep your voice down. Mama is
trying to get some rest. And Faith and I did not have sex."

"Why not?" Ivy asks, not looking at me as she tosses her
skateboard down with a clatter.

"I just get the feeling she'll want to wait."

"Or maybe not. Maybe she's just waiting for you to bust a move," Ivy says back, but when she sees the look on my face, she throws her hands up like she'll lay off.

I turn on my lamp, and we change focus. My application is due soon.

But I think about what Faith told me. Think about the fact that maybe I don't even want to go to MIT at all. That's just what I've been told I should want, so it was what I told myself I wanted, too.

Now I don't even know what I want anymore.

If I even want to go on living my life without Tyler. Why do I get to live while he's gone?

So instead of putting myself through that, the three of us play some NBA 2K Blacktop for a couple hours.

●

When I walk into the kitchen, I see Mama sitting at the table, and my nose gets a huge whiff of macaroni and cheese that might be on the verge of burning.

"Hey, honeybunches," she says to me. She seems distracted.

I slide into the seat across from her. "What's going on?"

"I got a call from a man today," she says. She looks at the stove, like she suddenly realizes the mac and cheese is burning. She gets up, turns off the stove, stirs the pot.

"Yeah? Who was it?"

She turns to face me, confusion on her face. "Someone from MIT."

My heart sinks. I haven't told her about any of this with MIT, because I could already tell how she'd react. She'd say I was crazy for applying to a place like that, a place that's so out of my league, a place where black boys don't belong.

I nod. "Oh. Yeah. What'd he want?"

"He asked for an update on your application. What's going on, Marvin?"

I take a deep breath. "I interviewed with him at the college fair, and he told me he'd recommend me as long as I send in my application, and I haven't done it yet. A part of me feels like I just can't even physically do it. Like I don't deserve to go after my dreams after everything, y'know?"

"You interviewed with MIT?"

"Yeah," I say, and wait for her yelling to start—but she just slips on a small smile and sits at the table, putting a hand on mine.

"That's great, honey."

"Really?"

She nods.

I swallow. "I don't even know if I want to go anymore. I mean, I feel like I've been told all my life that MIT's the best school if you're serious about science, but I don't know if that's just a lie I've been forced to believe. I've been thinking of applying to an HBCU instead, if they're even still taking applications."

"Really? Which one?"

I feel the weight being taken off my shoulders. "Howard."

Her smile makes me think she's excited for me, and we both stay quiet for a moment, just looking at each other, and then she gets up from the table and walks around to me and hugs me tight and tells me that she's proud of me.

And then she goes back to finishing up dinner, but I know that deep down she's probably feeling a hundred different things. Like how Tyler will never be able to apply to college now.

· 30 ·

DATE: JANUARY 15, 2019

TO: MARVIN D. JOHNSON (MY SON)
FROM: JAMAL P. JOHNSON
PRISON NUMBER: 2076-14-5555
MESSAGE:
Son,
   I've been thinking a lot about
freedom.
   What does freedom mean?

Who gets to be free?

Is someone free when they don't have to think about the way people look at them or treat them because of the color of their skin?

Is someone free when they don't have to spend time on this earth with people who have hearts made of hate?

Or is someone only really free when they're no longer a part of this world?

I don't know the answers. But I can only hope that Tyler is free, wherever he is, and that you can find your freedom, too.

I know you're hurting. Hell. I'm hurting, but never forget that I love you.

Daddy

I've started a social media page for Tyler on just about every site possible. The Facebook page has over five thousand likes. The Twitter page has over two thousand followers. Even Lance Anderson is following the Tumblr.

I check each page every day, monitoring what everyone's saying about Tyler, in an attempt to preserve his legacy. He was a good kid and he wanted things out of life—even things that he never told anyone. That's part of being a person. He wasn't a thug who deserved to die, and I make sure everyone remembers that every day.

I'll never forget Tyler.

I don't want the world to either.

●

I've already missed the MIT deadline, and I guess Mr. Ross has figured out that I'm not the right fit after all, because he stops calling, stops e-mailing. I check the Howard University website. The deadline is February 15—one month from now. One month to get my shit together. One month to get into the new school of my dreams.

I grab the box of Oatmeal Creme Pies and get started.

●

I text Ivy and G-mo that I'm going to the park with Faith. For today to be this nice out, the park is pretty empty. I sniff. The air smells like burnt rubber or fresh asphalt and paint. I look down to see that they've painted new lines on the court.

"Look, somebody left their ball," Faith says, pointing at a basketball on the court. She runs over to grab it. She dribbles the ball through her legs and around her body.

I follow her. "You play?" I ask.

"I love basketball," she answers. "When I was in school, I was on the team. Varsity all the way since the seventh grade." Every day I learn something new about her. I just hope I can keep up.

"Wanna play a game real quick?"

She swoops past me and lays it up, her fingertips almost touching the rim when she jumps. "Sure," she says, and winks.

We're the same height, and I can't even do what she just did. Damn.

She chucks me the ball.

I just dribble, standing still in my red basketball shorts and matching T-shirt. I stare at her, looking her up and down, like I'm challenging her. She looks hella beautiful in her white basketball shorts. I almost forget I'm dribbling, and she goes in for the steal.

"Hey, that wasn't fair!" I play-shout. "Foul!"

"Don't get distracted," she yells with a laugh as she goes in for another layup.

G-mo and Ivy arrive, hopping off their bike and skateboard.

"Yo, yo, yo," G-mo shouts. "'Sup, Faith. 'Sup, Marvin."

"'Sup, G," I say. "'Sup, Ivy."

They both hug me and it feels warm and amazing and I didn't know I needed them, but it clears my mind.

"Yo. I brought liquid oxygen," G-mo says, setting down bottles of cheap spring water.

Ivy puts down her water bottle and takes off her gray beanie, and I see her head is shaved. It looks like she went into the barbershop and asked for a straight-up low fade.

"Oh my God!" I say. "You shaved your head?"

She laughs. "It was a bet from a girl I'm talking to," Ivy says. "I clearly lost it."

Faith walks up to Ivy, examining her new haircut. "I love it," Faith tells her. "It's cute."

Ivy smiles like she's going to blush. "Thanks, guys." She takes off her jacket but keeps her sweatpants on.

"Who's ready to get their butt beat in some two on two?" G-mo goes, pulling his black shorts down out of his crotch area.

"Whatever," Ivy says.

"You're about to take this L," I say.

"Hell yeah," Faith goes.

"A'ight, let's do me and you, Faith, versus Marvin and Ivy?"

Faith says, "I'm down."

"Let's do it," Ivy yells. "Our ball!"

After a few games, the four of us sit down on the hot asphalt, stretching our legs, G-mo to my right and Faith at my left, Ivy on the other side of G-mo.

Ivy starts to sing the theme song of *A Different World*. G-mo and I join in.

"Okay. Literal LOL. What the hell was that?" Faith laughs, giving us the side-eye.

The three of us just laugh. And I didn't even realize how much I needed this moment.

We end up talking about nothing, about bullshit, until G-mo tells us he's got something to say.

"Yeah? What's up?" I go.

He takes a breath. "I've been thinking a lot about the whole college thing lately."

"Uh-huh?" me and Ivy say.

"I think I'm going to apply to UCLA. It's too late for the fall. So maybe for the spring."

"That's what's up, bro," Ivy says, fist-bumping him.

"You're a goddamn brilliant bastard," I tell him. "You're going to get in."

"You know, I'm looking into some local community colleges," Ivy says. "I really want to get into engineering."

I can't help but smile right now.

"That's so cool, yo," G-mo says, leaning back into the sand and dirt surrounding the court.

"Yeah, maybe I'll get my dream job with NASA or something. Who knows?" Ivy continues, gesturing with her hands to show the potentially endless possibilities. G-mo gives her dap.

There's a short pause. "I applied to Howard," I tell them, and they all look at me with surprise.

"So you're not applying to MIT anymore?" G-mo asks.

I shake my head.

"Having second thoughts?" Faith asks.

"Yeah," I say. "I realized I was only interested in going to MIT because all my life in school I was taught that MIT and other really prestigious, mostly white schools meant success. It meant acceptance. It meant that you were finally somebody in the world. When Dodson didn't even believe in me and said I had no chance of getting into MIT, I wanted to do any- and everything to prove him wrong." I stop to take a breath and look up at the pale, milky-blue sky. "I've spent too much time wondering what people think of me and spent so long trying to look good enough for Dodson, for white people, for Mama, for everyone except myself. And I think..." I look down at my feet. "I think it's my time to finally be who I am, who *I* want to be."

There's a moment of silence, except for the birds chirping in the trees in the distance.

"Man," G-mo says interrupting the quiet. "I feel you."

My eyes meet his and he nods at me.

We play one more game, changing up the teams, and then Faith drives us to get dinner at Tyler's favorite chicken and ribs joint, and I try not to hurt, even though I probably always will.

· 31 ·

The hateful-hot sun beams down like it's a UFO that's claiming me as its newest abductee. And I shield my face as best I can with my hand, but it doesn't seem to work. In the car, Faith chooses just the right station, landing on Tupac's "How Do U Want It." And my mind clears steadily.

And suddenly, all I can think about, all that is running through my mind, is *firsts*. My first time hearing the sound of a gun, my first time feeling loss, my first time meeting my best friends, my first time without a brother, my first time seeing bigotry, my first time being told I was not good enough, my first time being told that I *was*—and *am*—good enough, my first kiss, my first boner, my first love. And in my thoughts, I go over all the other firsts I'll get to experience with Faith.

We go over to her place for some alone time, and she puts on some music. When she sits down, she kisses me nice and quick on the lips. Her lips are soft—so soft, like touching cotton candy or like falling face-first on a mound of powdery snow. It's pretty fucking magical.

I kiss her mouth, her eyelids, her eyebrows, her forehead, her neck, her ears, and even her breasts through the fabric of her cheetah-print shirt. We roll down the couch and flip over. I'm on top, then she is on top, and then we flip again, and we are both on our sides, and this couch is so small and is ruining things for me. She darts up, squeezing my hand. "Wanna go to my bedroom? There's a lot more space in there."

"Yeah," I say without hesitation, following her.

We fall into the bed, and she pushes the covers to the side.

"You're the greatest," she says between kisses. "I like you so much."

"And I really, really, really like you back," I say to her, sucking on her bottom lip.

"Let's take our clothes off," she suggests.

And I have a two-second crisis with myself. I've never done this before. And I wonder if she knows.

"Sure, we can," I say, my mouth still so close to hers.

This is going to be awkward. I don't know what to do, and she's about to find out. Do I take my own clothes off? Or hers? I think she realizes now that I'm a fucking amateur. And so we end up doing a little bit of both—taking each other's clothes off, and our own.

In seconds, our skin is touching, bare bodies showing, chests heaving, and heat waving in between us. We're pressed so close together I damn near need a condom.

Then we are all hands and moans, and everything feels electrically charged, raging at full speed. She doesn't care where her hands go, and neither do I.

She reaches into a box underneath her bed and comes up with a condom. "Just to be on the safe side," she says, "put this on."

I bite open the package and slip it on after reading the back of it for directions.

"Are you sure?" I ask her.

She smiles and nods. "Yeah."

Everything picks up to full speed.

Our bodies touch and collide.

And we are one.

Feeling each other through and through.

I kiss her on the neck, and she lets out a moan that sends me kissing her. I look at her face and her expression is just fucking...everything, her eyes closed and her teeth making imprints on her bottom lip. And suddenly, I can almost feel all the layers that I have grown over my own purity stripping away. I feel them peel faster, the faster things move, the further things go.

· 32 ·

Two more weeks slide past, and we're suddenly only days away from the trial. They're going to have me and other people testify. I just hope that the jury listens and does the right thing.

Mama, still smelling like hard work and cigarette smoke, cleans out Tyler's room. The pain on her face causes me an intolerable amount of agony, and it takes a herculean effort to blink away the tears when she asks for my help. We take down his posters and put them in a box. We clean out his dresser drawers and nightstand, pulling out old sports magazines, a couple of condoms, a jar of Vaseline, and an application to community college that's half filled out, and this gets Mama to start crying. We strip the bed down and put the comforter, sheets, and pillowcases in a laundry basket for washing, eventually for slipping into the attic with other lost things.

"It still doesn't feel real," Mama says. "It feels like at any moment, he'll be coming home."

I blink, piling up all of his sports collection cards from a little stool in the corner of the room. I reach underneath the stool, and hidden there is a piece of paper held up by tape. It takes a few seconds, but I carefully peel back all the tape to see what it is.

"I try to make myself think that he'll be stumbling through the door asking me to make him a meal any day."

"Yeah," I say, "I feel that sometimes, too." I notice that I can talk about him, finally, without instantly losing my breath, or bursting into tears or flames.

"That's right," she says, folding up pairs of his socks and tossing them in the same laundry basket. "It helps me to think about it that way. I just wish…" Her voice trails off for a moment, and when I turn around, I see she has her hands placed against the wall. "I wish people knew who he really was. A boy with a big heart."

I unfold the paper and read it to myself. It's a letter. It's addressed to Dad, written in cursive, and in it Tyler tells about how much he's going to try to be the opposite of him when he grows up, about how much he hates Dad for what he did, about being afraid of Dad, and I have to stop reading, because it pains me to hold on to such a thing.

And I feel something in my chest. And it wants me to act on it.

I rip the letter to pieces and toss them in the trash bin, trying my best to forget that the letter ever happened, 'cause it makes me feel kind of shitty for not listening.

Tyler wrote Dad, and I wasn't alone.

Mama keeps on keeping on with picking apart his room, until it's nothingness, until it's bare, until all that is left is a mattress and a bed frame and a box in the corner filled with all the tangible things we'll remember about him.

Tyler was like our dad in many ways. He was hardheaded. He was stubborn. He was selfish. He was all of these most of the time. Tyler was a good kid, with dreams and goals for the future. Tyler was not a monster. And man, goddamn, it's so fucking sad to me how none of this mattered seconds before he was shot.

Tyler once looked up to Dad. Tyler looked up to me, and it's finally hitting me that I was too stupid to notice. And now, more than ever, I'm looking forward to the trial, where I'll let the world know just how good of a kid and brother he was.

At dinnertime, Mama has everyone over for a big feast before the school year ends, using money she's gotten from donations after Tyler's death. She sets up an extra seat for Tyler and everything. She even scrapes up enough money to buy streamers and balloons, so it really looks like a legit celebration, like a toast for the survivors of the hood or something, and as much as I feel sick, I go with it.

She makes fried chicken, mashed potatoes, and corn on the cob. There's something special about all of this—sitting here with her, Faith, G-mo, Ivy. I'm mended for a while.

At night, after everyone leaves, I toss and turn in bed. That's the new normal for me. I can't sleep, and I wouldn't be surprised if a doctor diagnosed me with insomnia for a lifetime. Some nights, I can't sleep because I transport myself in the memories of Tyler. Sometimes, it's like I hear him dribbling a basketball outside my window, shouting about how he's going to play for the Warriors alongside Steph Curry, dribbling like he's a mallet and the earth is a bass drum.

Tyler is gone, but the memories are not. And I'm okay with staying wide awake just to relive them.

· **33** ·

School has finally let out, which means we've got seventy-something days to enjoy ourselves before college, and we're just days from graduation. Auntie Nicola used to say that with graduation comes the real world, a handful of babies, and a string of life crises.

And this means I have weeks, no, maybe days to hear back about an admissions decision from Howard.

Ivy calls and tells me that she was accepted into all four colleges she applied to, and it's just a matter of her committing to one. She doesn't want to stray too far from Candace, her new girlfriend, who's already enrolled in a local beauty school.

And even G-mo tells me that he put in his application to UCLA and is pending late admission. It turns out the girl he's talking to has some sort of connection with the head honcho over there, like an aunt or uncle or cousin or something, and his chances of getting in have, like, doubled.

Faith is going to transfer to an art school in New York with a full-ride scholarship, which she earned by submitting one of her completely original and beautiful magazine collages. I promise her that I'll come to visit. I'm going to find a way to make this happen. Maybe after the trial, I'll be able to think a bit straighter.

All this to say: My two best friends, and my girlfriend, have committed to their futures, made promises to their dreams, and I still feel stuck with no plan A, just a plan B titled *Hood Life Forever* weighing down on my shoulders.

●

My birthday is coming up soon, and I make it a thing to let everyone know that I will not celebrate it. I can't. It's not a happy day like it used to be. It's more of a day of mourning— a day where we'll just gather to grieve and cry over a marble cake. Knowing that this will be a year of many firsts without the other half of the equation has me numb with grief.

I've got over five hundred followers on Tumblr now and a shit-ton of reblogs, and according to G-mo, who suddenly claims to be an expert on Tumblr, this is big—like, really big. More people are listening. And every day, the like count on Facebook climbs higher and higher. We're at nine thousand right now.

I'm trying to sort out which photo to upload to all the pages next. I try to keep them synchronized and updated. Yesterday, I discovered some pictures of the protest, so I just reposted them. My goal has been to post something to remember him daily.

I can't decide if I want to post this photo of Tyler and me when we were four, the two of us sitting on Mama's and Dad's laps in some strip mall, the Easter bunny making the peace sign behind us—the two of us looking absolutely terrified by the giant rabbit. Tyler would wrestle me to the ground if he ever knew I was thinking about posting this. Wherever he is, I know he's looking down on me, cussing me out under his breath. But probably with a smile, too.

●

It still takes effort to get up out of bed.

Some days, when I do, I just stare at the blackness I see in the mirror hanging on my closet door. I tell myself that I love this skin, that I've always loved my blackness, that if the world doesn't love me, I will love myself for the both of us. After reminding myself that I matter, that I always mattered, that Tyler mattered and still does, I make a promise to myself. I promise that I'll never be silent about things that matter, that I'll keep on saying his name for the rest of my days.

Blasting "I Got 5 On It" by Luniz on my phone and eating an Oatmeal Creme Pie, I walk outside to check the mail. Today's a nice day, and it doesn't look like it's going to be miserably rainy at all, which goes against everything my weather app promised.

One whiff of the air and I can tell somebody's having a cookout somewhere nearby. I don't know exactly where it's coming from, but it smells good as hell. I can even hear the faint bass of music in the distance over my own.

I pull three envelopes from the mailbox. One of them is addressed to me. It's from Howard. A gasp slips out of me, and I damn near do the Dougie in the middle of the street. I'm not going to open it right now. I'm going to go inside first and show Mama.

I'm cat daddying all the way up the driveway.

"Mama!" I shout, bursting through the door.

The thump of my heart gets even louder when I set foot in the living room, where she's cleaning up—vacuum going, bleach water sitting in a bucket, gospel music blaring and everything.

"Look, look, look!" I shout to her, waving the envelope in her face.

Her eyes get wide. She takes off her yellow cleaning gloves and hugs me. "Open it, open it," she says, damn near jumping up and down for me.

I don't even care about being all neat. I rip the shit out of the envelope and pull out a letter. At the top it says: CONGRATULATIONS! ADMITTED! And I don't even catch myself crying until Mama's wiping my tears for me.

She reads the letter out loud, then says, "I'm so proud of you." She steps back and just smiles at me, like she's finally scraped up a little happiness.

I hug her again and everything feels perfect.

●

Wednesday comes, and I'm in the passenger seat in the car with Mama, and we're spending all of today together at her request. She's driving us to some burger place she found by her job. I stare out the window at the rapidly passing scenery, jamming to an oldie, "Doo Wop (That Thing)" by Lauryn Hill, on the radio. I guess all of this is to ease our nerves about the grand jury trial happening in a matter of days. Just days now. *Man, it's so close.* I try not to think about the trial, because I know that in the end, it doesn't matter what the jury decides. Tyler's life still mattered, even if they can't see it for themselves.

When we pull up to a little burger shack with an orange sign in front of the door that says IN-N-OUT BURGER, Mama cuts the engine, and the music cuts off right at the chorus, leaving an awkward silence.

Inside the burger joint, the air smells like onions, and it's fairly empty, so all the staff members are looking at us. Mama orders a plain cheeseburger, and I get the double-double.

We both eat slowly once we choose a table. I can tell she wants to talk by how she watches me take every bite. That's a thing about her I've picked up over the years.

"How's your food?" I ask.

"Pretty good," she says, dipping fries in ketchup.

"Yeah." I nod, going in for my fries now.

There's a beat before she clears her throat. She pushes a piece of hair away from her face and pins it back into her short ponytail. "I've been thinking about scattering Tyler's ashes," she says, looking down at her food. "Nicola said it's a good thing, too."

What. The. Hell?

Faintly, very faintly, I let out a breath. I don't know

whether to be mad or not, but I'm mad and sad and hurt all at once. All I say back is "Why?"

It looks like she wants to scream or cry or both. "I just thought maybe it would be good for us."

"*Us?*" I question.

"You and me. Tyler, too," she responds. "I don't think it's right for me to be holding on to him forever, baby." She wipes her mouth with a napkin. "I've been thinking about some good places to do it at. Like maybe a river or ocean or something. Somewhere that it feels right."

I just nod and finish up my food, trying to process everything. I think about it on the way back home, think about it all night. When I go to sleep, I end up dreaming about it, too.

· 34 ·

Marvin. Marvin!" Mama's standing over me, trying to wake me up. My eyelids are low, but I blink them to focus. "It's time to get up, baby. We got somewhere to be." It's Saturday and Mama's talking about how she found the perfect place to scatter Tyler's ashes.

I get out of bed, go pee, brush my teeth, and then change into some clean clothes—nothing too fancy. Something comfortable. It's going to be pretty hot today, so I choose some shorts and a shirt.

In the kitchen, Mama is waiting on me while eating eggs.

There's a plate across from her with just toast with grape jelly, no eggs. She knows how much I hate them. I sit down and she starts going on and on about the Sterling Point Estuary, and how she thinks it's the most peaceful place in all of Alabama to put him, about how Auntie Nicola thinks so, too.

I don't even finish a whole piece of toast before she's done eating.

She goes to get Tyler's urn and the photo book she made. She pulls out a picture of the last family reunion we had. Tyler and I were three. Still babies, as Mama would say. She doesn't even break down crying in front of me. She just holds it up to her heart. This is progress.

We pick up G-mo and Ivy from their places on our way to the Sterling Point Estuary, which is just a strait separating three different cities far away from Sterling Point, and it takes what feels like hours to get here. Faith meets up with us.

The sun is blazing hot, quails and pelicans greeting us in the sky as we walk to the edge of the riverbank, taking slow steps on a wooden strip. I've been tasked with carrying Tyler's urn. I've never hated anything more than this feeling of carrying Tyler, I mean, his ashes, no, I mean, Tyler.

It's him, but it's not.

My head throbs. I don't know if I can do this. *Breathe in,* I tell myself. *Then out.*

Everyone's quiet, and all I can hear is nature—the birds, the water swishing around, the fish making bubbles in it. The sound of cars way back on the road is faint in the distance.

Ivy and G-mo take turns patting me on the back, reminding me that everything's okay. I try to simmer my stomach and prepare myself for what might be the hardest thing I'll ever have to do in my life.

Faith gets close to me. "How're you feeling?" she asks. This question really could be answered in a bunch of different ways right now.

If I say I'm okay, I'd be lying to her and to myself. I sigh. "This just feels weird." I spent last night reading all about scattering ashes. It's supposed to be a big step in the grief journey. It doesn't seem like it, though. At least, not yet.

"Just close your eyes, if it helps," she says, popping her gum.

"I'm trying. It's just seriously hard." I'm staring at my reflection in the water now, Tyler clutched to my chest.

"God, my baby," Mama says, wiping her eyes.

I exhale.

It feels like the world leaps forward without me.

"You got this, Marv," Ivy says.

"Stay strong," G-mo adds.

It's nice to have them here. Sometimes it seems like I hold them back from being amid all the fun, like they are my own personal wallflowers with no perks. But it's been reassuring to learn that we can be there for one another in all the ways we need, and we'll be okay with it.

Pac said it best in his song "Until the End of Time." He said, *In the hood, true homies make you feel good.* That's something I need to remember.

Ivy and G-mo are true homies.

I walk down a little bit more to get closer to the edge. I kneel and run a hand through the water. It's warm. And I know he'll like it.

I wait for the wind to settle down, painful seconds slipping past. Then I twist off the lid of the urn, gasping and blinking back tears.

I nod at G-mo. Then Ivy. Then Faith. Then Mama.

Everything feels like it's moving in slow motion. I take another breath and begin pouring the ashes into the water, watching them float and then sink and disperse.

"How are you feeling now?" Faith asks, her hand on my back.

"All right." It's a sad kind of *all right*, though. Tears are streaming down my face and the wind returns, carrying him farther and farther away. Almost instantly, it's open season for tears. It's an all-you-can-care-to-cry feast among us. I hug Faith, then G-mo, then Ivy, and then Mama. And then we are all hugging one another at the same time.

I look up at the sky after we break apart and see the sun

moving out from behind a bunch of clouds. I don't know where Tyler is, but I know he'll always be a part of my present and my future. I can faintly hear his voice thanking me for letting him go.

I'll never forget what happened. I'll never forget that my twin was once here and then brutally taken out of my life, leaving behind an awful, sinking hole inside me, paining me empty. I'll never forget our memories. One day, I'll see him again. But until then, I just have to keep reminding everyone around me that his life matters.

ACKNOWLEDGMENTS

First and foremost, thank you to my Lord and savior, Jesus Christ, for getting me through all the tears that were shed while writing this book.

Special, special thanks to all the folks who made this book possible:

Lauren Abramo, my wonderful, brilliant, hardworking, and championing superhero agent and friend. From the first time I queried you, you championed me and this book and fought so hard for it. From the very moment we first talked on the phone and I heard you gush about my book, I knew you would be the best agent.

Kheryn Callender, you are such a phenomenal and talented editor, and you have made this book so, so much stronger. You got skills for real. I'm humbled and honored to have worked with you for so many months to shape my book to be its very best. Thank you for getting me. Thank you for getting my book. Thank you for you.

Big ups to the fantastic team at Dystel, Goderich & Bourret, especially Michael, Jim, and Sharon. Thanks for championing my book behind the scenes as much as you all have.

Huge, HUGE thank-yous to everyone at Little, Brown Books for Young Readers, especially Alvina Ling, Kristina Pisciotta, Jessica Shoffel, Jennifer McClelland-Smith, Elizabeth Rosenbaum, Elena Yip, Victoria Stapleton, Michelle Campbell, and Marisa Finkelstein. Your enthusiasm and encouragement throughout the publication of *Tyler Johnson Was Here* has been amazing, and I'm so grateful to have you all as part of my team.

Thanks to Charlotte Day and Marcie Lawrence for creating such a gorgeous, poignant, and powerful cover for *Tyler Johnson Was Here*. I have all the soft boy feels. Seriously, I'm so, so happy and lucky to have this cover.

To my name-twin and best friend, Jay Elliot Flynn, thank you for supporting me, for your insight, for always being there when I need you most, and for reading *Tyler Johnson Was Here* when I first wrote it, back when it was four hundred messy, messy pages. You're a real G. I'm proud to know you.

My ride-or-die best friends, Reggie, Deyon, Rajj, Zach W., Zach S., Mitch, Jacob, and Chris. I love each and every one of you and value your friendship. Thank you for being by my side throughout the highs and lows of finishing this book.

Thank you to Carl Frost and Neil Kring for being two of

the best pastors who have supported me through this journey. I love you both and value your friendship.

My Revo Squad, thank you all for always encouraging me to keep going and to reach greater heights. I couldn't have finished without your affirmation and friendship.

Adi Alsaid, Laura Silverman, Angie Thomas, Nic Stone, Dhonielle Clayton, L.L. McKinney, Adrianne Russell, Brandy Colbert, Justina Ireland, Ibi Zoboi, Phil Stamper, Dave Connis, Jeff Zentner, Becky Albertalli, Farrah Penn, Tomi Adeyemi, Tiffany D. Jackson, Simon Curtis, Elsie Chapman, Eric Smith, Heidi Heilig, Hannah Moskowitz, Marieke Nijkamp, Adam Silvera, John Corey Whaley, and Kara Thomas, among many, many author friends who were the best support system I could ask for going into this new world of publishing.

Thanks to my family and loved ones who have cheered behind the scenes since I finished this book, especially my two sisters, Diamond and Taya. I love you two and can't wait to see you both conquer the world someday.